I Meant It Once

I Meant It Once

stories

Kate Doyle

ALGONQUIN BOOKS
OF CHAPEL HILL
2023

Published by
ALGONQUIN BOOKS OF CHAPEL HILL
Post Office Box 2225
Chapel Hill, North Carolina 27515-2225

an imprint of Workman Publishing Co., Inc.
a subsidiary of Hachette Book Group, Inc.
1290 Avenue of the Americas
New York, New York 10104

Printed in the United States of America.
Design by Steve Godwin.

The publisher is not responsible for websites (or their content)
that are not owned by the publisher.

This is a work of fiction. While, as in all fiction,
the literary perceptions and insights are based on experience,
all names, characters, places, and incidents either are products
of the author's imagination or are used fictiously.

Some of the stories in this book originally appeared in the following publications: *ANMLY*
("Cinnamon Baseball Coyote"); *Bodega* ("That Is Shocking"); *Cordella Magazine* ("Briefly"
[as "I Went Briefly Abroad"]); *Electric Literature* ("Moments Earlier"); *Meridian* ("At the Time");
No Tokens ("This Is the Way Things Are Now"); *Pigeon Pages* ("We Can't Explain");
A Public Space ("Hello It's You" [as "We'll Be Alone"]); *Split Lip Magazine* ("The Goldfish
in the Pond at the Community Garden"); *Wigleaf* ("I Figured We Were Doomed").

Library of Congress Cataloging-in-Publication Data

Names: Doyle, Kate, 1990- author.
Title: I meant it once : stories / Kate Doyle.
Description: First edition. | Chapel Hill, North Carolina :
Algonquin Books of Chapel Hill, 2023. |
Summary: "A collection of short stories in which young women search for ways to break free
from the expectations of others and find a way to be in the world"—Provided by publisher.
Identifiers: LCCN 2023005422 | ISBN 9781643752815 (trade paperback) |
ISBN 9781643755267 (ebook)
Subjects: LCGFT: Short stories.
Classification: LCC PS3604.O95487 I33 2023 |
DDC 813/.6—dc23/eng/20230206
LC record available at https://lccn.loc.gov/2023005422

10 9 8 7 6 5 4 3 2 1
First Edition

CONTENTS

I Meant It Once

That Is Shocking

——— —— ———

This happened to me when I was still in college. It was winter, dark, a new semester. Valentine's Day, no less.

I remember that night, in the aftermath, I put on my coat and walked the four blocks between my dorm and Tom's, in the extreme cold, to relate the events as they had transpired. Tom said, That is shocking, and sat me on his dorm-room twin bed. He produced blue Kleenex after blue Kleenex until I had somewhat calmed down.

I said to Tom, Maybe if the scones had not been heart-shaped? I would not feel so, I don't know.

A few days later, my friend Charlotte came across a red, heart-shaped cookie cutter. She'd been digging around for a packet of instant hot chocolate in the kitchen of the campus literary house where she and I were roommates. She

found the heart-shape jumbled in a drawer of various uten-
sils, and she brought it to the dining room to peer at me
through its empty center. I was sitting with my homework
and hers fanned around me on the table, and she said, with
a blurted, wry laugh: Margaret, do you know what this
cookie cutter would be *great* for making?

Shh, I said, looking around—because *he* lived there, too.
But Charlotte could not stop laughing. She had the kind of
laugh you wanted to be part of. People in the living room
looked over at us.

At the time, I thought I understood the lesson in this story:
namely, if you decide to end things with someone on the
grounds you are too busy to see her, then materializing to
say so with a plateful of heart-shaped scones you've spent
the entirety of an afternoon preparing may fail to suggest
the fullness of your schedule.

I was in a literature class that semester called Self and
Others, which is how I'd met Tom, who was a poet. I loved
walking with Tom across the quad after class, trying on
his snarky opinions, the sun on our faces. Tom said, Let
us begin a collaboration of mournful lyric essays, com-
piled from incidents like this one of yours, and each one
will conclude *that is shocking*! He added, I wasn't going
to say so in case it all worked out, but honestly, he's marginally shorter than you, and definitely going a little bald

at the age of nineteen. So let's not proceed as if he were a loss.

I thought this was unkind and very funny. But I said how it was not about loss, rather about humiliation, about being treated as disposable, about human decency, and also how it isn't fair to tell a person that you're "breaking up" in those words precisely when you have not, in fact, really been dating—you have only done things like make out in the back stairwell of the literary society dorm, the stairwell where we kept the communal vacuum cleaner, a stairwell, he told me, "no one ever uses," which did not even turn out to be true. Natalie from the third floor had appeared, descending, on her way to make oatmeal cookies in the kitchen. I had been unable to disentangle my feet from the hose of the vacuum.

It is such a stupid story, of course—but it is one of those that stays with you, I could not let it go. Frenetic, intent, I was known in those years for being tightly wound. Calm down, people would say to me. There is still, at this college I went to, a hole in the wall of an obscure corner of the English department, kicked there by me. That's unrelated to this particular story, but illustrative of how I was then. What got me about the heart scones is how I had not anticipated it—was unable to stop it.

Whereas other people seemed able to end their romantic things more skillfully, more tidily.

Take Charlotte: she'd been sort of seeing this friend of ours, Jamey, and though they were no longer really together, they were still friends, and he still came around. No problem. She was always telling me how they felt very cool, at ease, and on the same page about things. In fact on this same infamous Valentine's Day I had seen them together in our kitchen, boiling water for pasta, heating marinara on the stovetop, and it had seemed to me impressively— enviably—normal and fine.

Stretched next to Tom on his bed, looking up at the ceiling, I remember saying how the worst part was this: after the text that said *Happy Valentine's, can I come over, I have a present for you*, and my text back *Oh thanks sure, see you soon*, I spent the intervening half hour feeling guilty, not having any Valentine to give in return. The sun was going down outside my window. Shadows lengthened on the parking lot. I remember I contemplated running to the college bookstore, in falling darkness, for a chocolate bar.

After we cleaned up my wrinkled clumps of tissue, strewn all around Tom's floor and bed, he said surely I had at least earned a bowl of chocolate soft-serve for my humiliation. So we crossed the quad to the dining hall where, under the high ceiling and fluorescent lights, we encountered Charlotte making a quesadilla in the Tastes of the World line. I always loved running into Charlotte, finding her in places outside our room where I had not expected her. She said, What's wrong, why do you look so sad? I said, I'm not sad, these are tears of indignation and rage, not tears of sadness. I am, sad-wise, unaffected.

The next time I ran into him, I said: I have your plate. But he said to me, with his warm smile, his backpack slung from one shoulder, Oh I just took that from the dining hall once. The plate is not so important to me, you can have it. I said, I am not really interested in keeping your plate, you are absolutely taking it home. So he obliged, and came down the hall, and waited in my open doorway for me to give it back.

Tom disapproved of my living in the literary house to begin with. I write poems, he said. I don't need to be in some club that confirms it, and neither do you. I remember he was sitting cross-legged on top of the washing machine, open notebook in his lap, and I was on the floor, trying to feed a handful of quarters to a jammed dryer. He started to compose some lines, saying: I'm writing an ode to a beautiful old house, where everyone living inside it is weird. Don't worry, he said. You're exempt. I laughed; I had the bright sense of being singled out.

Listen, I remember saying to Charlotte, one night in our room. Using the term "breakup" when you are explicitly not dating is like saying you're abandoning your career in the ballet definitively when actually you've only been to class two to four times ever in your life, and all those times you just talked about how you really weren't sure about ballet. Charlotte peeled back the covers of her bed. She said, You said this to me yesterday. I said, I did? She said, There are worse things in life than your scones, you know.

Of course I know that, I said. Of course I know.

It was like I could not stop telling the story. Reactions tended to divide: Many agreed that the scones were tainted, a betrayal. Others would say, But perfectly good scones, Margaret! And you didn't even eat them? On the night when Charlotte found the heart-shaped cookie cutter, our friend Jamey was there again—the one Charlotte had sort of been dating, though now they were only friends. He was working on his honors thesis in French translation at the far end of the table, and he said, one elbow planted in the spread-open spine of a book, pen slid behind his ear: One question, were they *good* scones? Charlotte slung the cookie cutter across the tabletop at him. She said, Margaret threw the scones in the garbage, of course, she threw them all away.

Jamey, contemplative, said, I don't know. Perfectly good scones? I might have eaten them.

Charlotte looked darkly into her cup of hot chocolate as Jamey asked me to clarify: What flavor were the scones? Which, of course, I couldn't say. He was partial to cranberry himself, he told us. I didn't take much offense to this compared to Charlotte, who made an excuse to go to the kitchen. Admittedly, I had always had sort of a thing for Jamey, so maybe I was forgiving. He had cut his hair and shaved his beard during a trip home over Presidents' Day. At the far end of the table, he frowned his new, clean-shaven frown over his French–English dictionary. I remember I lifted the heart-shape and looked at him through it.

Sometimes in retrospect I can't make sense of myself. Like how in the moments the scones were being foisted on me— one lamp lit on my desk, and the sun setting red outside my window behind the dark, bare trees lined up on the far side of the parking lot, branching like veins against the sky—I kept picking up the plate while he was talking and trying to give the scones back, then thinking this was petulant and setting them back down. I was at one end of the bed and he sat at the other, close to the door. He still wore his coat. He had one hand easily grasping the bedpost. The whole room was lit beautifully, warm and aglow. Outside, the dusky sky shaded soft, electric blue, and I was like a puppet with this plate, just lifting it off the dresser and returning it to the dresser, again and again and again and again.

I remember him saying to me once with merry concern, taking his hands out of my hair: I'm not looking to be with someone, like in a dating sense. We were just inside the doorway to the abandoned common room. Late January, 3 a.m.—in one corner the artificial Christmas tree still stood, plugged in and blinking. My cardigan flung, heaped and shadowy, on the floor.

But surely, said Tom, all this merits inclusion in the collected *That Is Shocking*. He also wanted to include my story about Robbie from the second floor, who used to lend me this soft crew-team sweatshirt of his I loved, who was always leaving notes on the whiteboard by my door, and who once took me on a much-anticipated date during which he talked mostly of an ex-girlfriend still in high school. That's icky, I remember saying to him then, pushing sushi around the dregs of my soy sauce—picturing this girl who did not yet have a driver's license, thinking that now I would have to give back the sweatshirt. Robbie said, It isn't, you don't even know her. He said, You don't know.

At one point, again putting down the scones, I said, You're too *busy* to keep seeing me? I was cognizant of being a little fixated on his fingers, washed in yellow lamplight where they held the bedpost. That semester he was chairman of Waffle Sundays at our literary house and a member of the Ultimate Frisbee team. I said, You're aware I'm busy, too? He said, in his friendly way, so benevolent, thoughtful: No, that's how busy I've been. Too busy to notice that you're busy.

Fuck that, said Tom, writing joyfully, as the dryer, finally, started to rumble. He said, I'm actually allotting a whole stanza for this guy.

I kept having to see him, because we both lived in that house. One morning, for example, I encountered him in the kitchen. It had snowed all night, and now it was sunny—a blinding, sparkly day. Light streaked in across the littered countertops: none of us washed our dishes here. He said, Oh Margaret, hey, I've been wanting to give you something. I refrained from saying, Whatever it is, please let it be shaped like a heart. He knelt and rooted in his backpack, and I watched the noon winter sun catch the bald part of his scalp, glow rosy in the soft rounds of his earlobes. Finally, he turned back and offered up to me, in his cupped hands, an ugly tangle of hairpins. Taken one by one from my hair, the night I'd stayed. Tenderly? They looked like bugs, clinging together this way. Ungracefully, I clawed them from his palms. Then he re-zipped his backpack while I considered that these hairpins had once been the source of an actual nice moment. How many of these do you *wear*? he'd said, incredulous, awed. So many, I said. He kissed my neck hungrily, affectionately, in the exquisite darkness of his room. I remember I felt a funny small thrill that we even knew each other, that we'd come from different places to meet at this place, in this time.

The fact is that within a few years, Jamey and I would end up living together in New York.

By then—for related reasons—Charlotte and I were no longer in touch.

On the day Jamey broke up with me in the kitchen of the apartment we'd shared for almost a year, I threw a glass into our sink, where it broke into pieces. Jamey looked disconcerted, highly embarrassed, as he picked the larger shards from the drain. The bright overhead lamp caught the broken points, the profusion of glittering fragments. I said, Tom and I swore years ago we'd write a book about terrible endings. I want you to know when I put you in it, I will be unforgiving.

Jamey had this big piece of glass pinched between his thumb and forefinger, his shirtsleeve rolled up. He said, Tom? I said, Unforgivable.

Tom had gone on to do sort of well, writing-wise. I would go see him do readings at bars. He won an obscure award for a chapbook he did, and a prize for a late revision of the old-house-weird-people poem. Drunk at a reading on the Lower East Side, not long after Jamey moved out, I pressed my hand to Tom's forearm and said, Remember our collaboration? He said he remembered the title being important, but that it escaped him now.

I put my empty beer glass down on the bar and said, That is shocking.

Holy shit, Tom said, That's amazing. He said, I really forgot.

We determined we would actually write it. We started meeting at my half-empty apartment on weekends. We would lie around on my bed drinking coffee, and he would write, and I would write, and we would compare our notes. Once, after I read a bit aloud about it being shocking that I'd started dating my best friend Charlotte's boyfriend Jamey in the first place, Tom said, face pressed to one of my pillows, Whatever happened to her? Are you still friends?

I said, You don't remember?

I felt humiliated and betrayed, is what I used to say about the scones—which is the kind of thing I imagined Charlotte might say to me now, if we ever ran into each other. Internet photos implied she, too, had moved to New York, like pretty much everyone we ever knew in college. Prior to my breakup with Jamey, I had invested significant mental energy inventing numberless unexpected, excruciating ways we might run into her—as, for example, we once encountered Robbie from the second floor on a Brooklyn-bound L. Pleasantries having been exchanged, Robbie had detailed his revived relationship with the girl from high school, now twenty-two.

Per our arrangement, Jamey came for his share of our belongings while I was not at home. He took the nightstand, the big plant, the most light-giving lamp. The blue ceramic French press that was actually mine. Most of what was hanging on our walls, though not the picture hooks, of course, which stayed behind: floating above the sofa, over the toilet, next to my nightstand. Dead center on the expanse of wall dividing living room from bedroom. Four of them, vertically, on the narrow strip of wall between kitchen and bathroom. One Sunday, Tom picked through all my bracelets and necklaces, which I was keeping in a bowl on the floor where the nightstand had been. He went around the apartment, draping his favorites from picture hooks—I'm trying to fill up all these weird gaps, he told me.

He moved some of my books into the spot where the plant had been.

One Sunday, at dusk, the sky turning red in the apartment windows, we needed more coffee. Tom brewed some and we watched it rise in the glass carafe of the inferior drip coffeemaker. I sat on the kitchen counter, in the shadow of the refrigerator, kicking my heels, one-two one-two, against the lower cabinets. I said, I should have known about Jamey the moment the words "perfectly good scones" passed his lips. I said, My litmus test going forward will be, anyone I'm inviting into my life in any way gets told the story—and only people who would not ever eat the scones are permitted anywhere near me. Friends, lovers, colleagues, I mean it.

Holy shit, I forgot about Scone Guy, said Tom, washing out a mug for himself. He said, I totally forgot.

He said, Do you ever feel weird this still bothers you?

He said, Where even is he these days?

I said, Let's pretend I'm the sort of person who wouldn't keep track of him.

It is possible by then I was crying. I took out my phone to text Jamey that the French press was mine, and I wanted it back. I wrote, *I can't wait until tomorrow. Bring it here now.* He wrote, *I've been drinking too much coffee Margaret, the French press is not so important to me.* He texted, *It's fine.* He said, *You can have it.*

Of course I can have it, I told him. *It's mine!* I said this last part out loud, too, and Tom's eyes widened, he looked at the floor. When Jamey didn't text back I dialed his number, which rang and rang and went to voicemail. I called a second time, a third time, the trill of the phone repeating in my ear. Just have some coffee, said Tom, and I ignored him. I paced the ransacked rooms of my apartment. Outside the windows, the sky grew dark, its color drained. I thought I might burst into flames.

I can't pick up the phone, Jamey texted finally. *Now's not a good time. I'm not going to come over there now,* he said. *Just calm down, okay?*

He said: *Take it easy.*

This Is the Way Things Are Now

— — —

1. Catherine and Helen: In high school they would sleep over in the same bed on weekends, watch old movies, sleep too late. Catherine would comment on Helen's sleep-talking in the mornings, and Helen would cover her ears and say: Don't tell me, don't tell me, I don't want to know.

2. Years later: Now they're twenty-two, and Catherine has this boyfriend she more or less lives with. So she is saying things like, Thank you for coming for the weekend, Helen, and here is your air mattress on the living-room floor.

3. Christmas she is twenty-two: Every year, their parents give Helen and Evan and Grace each a tree ornament, meant to commemorate some accomplishment in the past year. What will mine be this time, says Helen, Congratulations, you're having a meltdown? Evan suggests, Congratulations, you work at a coffee shop, as a possible alternative.

4. Amends: Helen calls Catherine on a morning in December that is strangely warm and sort of raining. She stands with her back to the shut-off fountain in Washington Square Park, looking down at her reflection spread around her in a murky slick of puddle. Catherine is glad to hear from her. Catherine appreciates that she's sorry for being a shitty, selfish friend—sorry for hating Catherine's boyfriend, for indulging how it feels to have a strong opinion. Please also tell Alexander I'm sorry, Helen says, Please tell him I'm sure he's actually a nice person. And though Catherine surely won't, she promises she will.

5. Catherine makes tentative conversation: She says, How is New York, how is living with your parents? I still can't believe they sold your house in Rye, I loved your house. On the other side of the fountain, a child falls in a puddle and lets out a whimper. Helen says, My father didn't want to keep commuting into the city from the suburbs. He said it was not worth his time.

6. Catherine says she and Alexander agree: When they have children, they won't raise them in the suburbs. And Helen really hates the way it feels to compare herself— e.g. My best friend Catherine lived much of her childhood in Prague; I for comparison grew up entirely in the suburbs of fucking Westchester—as if this is the whole point of Catherine, to stand in contrast. Nevertheless the fact remains, Helen has no idea where she will raise her children, if she ever has them. She may not even want them.

7. **Catherine, standing in contrast:** She seems possessed of a striking certainty with regards to her theoretical children, especially for someone who used to say in high school, I mostly just hope I have many, many affairs.

8. **All-consuming:** Catherine, age fifteen, twirls the spoon around her coffee mug and says, In at least one of my affairs, I'll throw a glass of water in his face, and that will be it, the end—I'll be gone. Privately Helen finds this enthralling, but she makes a face to imply it sounds silly. Catherine looks out the window and says: I'd also like one to happen somewhere on the Mediterranean Sea.

9. **For old times' sake:** In their hometown in the suburbs north of New York, there are sprinklers set to timers on the athletic fields behind the high school. It is Catherine who suggests they run through them, on a night in May when they are seventeen, and it is Catherine who wants to do it again when they are twenty-one, though these days they are talking less and less. Helen from the passenger seat says, No way definitely not, because Catherine in the car has just said this thing about wanting to have eventual babies with Alexander, and Helen is not at all interested in acting out some pretense of frolic on a football field. Anyway, then it starts to rain.

10. What Helen's mother says about her: You were always very set in your ways.

11. What Helen's mother says about Evan: Why does it matter that we always said he was better at acting than you? Couldn't we let him have one thing to be better at?

12. Evan and Grace and Helen's tree ornaments, respectively: The Eiffel Tower, for studying abroad; a squash racquet, self-explanatory; and a coffee cup. You're working very hard there, says her father. We want to recognize that.

13. Catherine's bed, in high school: It's worn and beautiful like an old cloth doll, and her sheets have a pattern of fading pink vines. She keeps black-and-white postcards taped to her wall, and when she shuts off the lamp, the light through the window from next door falls over both Catherine and Helen's long hair on their pillows. In the mornings, they eat toast in Catherine's bed.

14. On a napkin during a slow day at Caffeine, Helen writes: *The tension between the past and present will ruin you.* Then she throws it away, because how prosaic. She doesn't know what else to do, so she cleans the espresso machine.

15. On the walk home from Caffeine: Helen always cries. This is a main feature of the meltdown she's had, is having, along with this bombed-out sensation in her chest all the time. I think I'm failing at everything and probably deserve to, she tells her parents one night. You're being far too hard on yourself, says her father. Her mother says, You're smart and you've had a lot of advantages in your life. We're hopeful you will find your way out of this somehow. (Which feels like saying, *You have no reason to be sad*.)

16. While the Gilmore Girls are fighting on television: Helen says, I've been thinking about my behavior and I'm sorry I have sometimes been a horrible, aloof sister. It is Grace's first night back and they are watching Netflix with the volume up too high. Grace says, I think you haven't really been horrible per se but thank you. She says, I really hate to see you this way. Helen turns her face into the cushions of the couch and starts crying, again. Can you move over please, says Grace.

17. Adjustment Disorder: It does sound like something you would have, the whole family agrees.

18. Grace's ex: They are making Christmas cookies when Grace says, I called him yesterday. Helen looks up from frosting a reindeer to ask, Why? Grace shakes green sprinkles on a wreath and says, While you were crying on the couch that one night, I was thinking about how difficult it is for me to be here for you. And that made me feel like I should thank him, for how he helped when I was going through my thing. Helen says, Wait what thing? Casually Grace replies, Oh—after Mom and Dad sold our house and moved back to the city, I was always walking around campus, just crying and crying. Just missing our house, the way things used to be. I was really crazy.

19. What their mother says about that: I always liked him. (Grace says, Thanks, we know actually.)

20. What Helen says: Why didn't you tell me? (Grace shrugs and says, I just didn't.)

21. What Catherine says on the phone: Poor Grace, that's sad.

22. Catherine's bed now: Is it as comfortable as the old one? Helen has no way of knowing.

23. Terrible fight on Christmas: You are always paddling against the fucking stream and it's exhausting for the rest of us, I mean get over yourself, says Evan, not even looking at Helen, and he throws the wooden spoon into the sink and huffs off to the living room. If this family doesn't stop fighting, says their father, sadly, and doesn't finish the sentence.

24. Their mother, not having this, says: Helen, put that spoon back where it goes please, now.

25. One thing to be better at: Evan is only going to be home for twelve days of his winter break anyway, after which he is going back to Middlebury to start rehearsals for a play—he has the leading role. Before the terrible fight, he and Helen both agree he should spend the whole time at Caffeine, learning his lines and letting her ply him with espresso drinks. One day he actually shows up. She makes him a macchiato, then another.

26. Meet-cute: Catherine drops her commuter pass getting off the Metro. Alexander dashes after her, up the stairs and down the block and into the stationery store in Dupont Circle, where she is looking for a birthday card. They go out for a glass of wine. He asks for her phone number.

27. What Helen never got that year: A birthday card. But how petulant to hold that particular grudge.

28. Birthdays: Catherine's is October 3 and Helen's is May 14. When Catherine turns seventeen, Helen brings cupcakes, and they sit on the front steps of school, and around them the air is just slightly too brisk. They drink coffee from the cafeteria, the sun warming the stone steps, the wind making the leaves bristle down the driveway. One day this will all seem very far away, says Catherine, while Helen is trying to light a candle and not succeeding. Helen smirks because how misty and all-knowing Catherine can make herself sound. In the end they leave a dozen dead matches piled on the steps and go back to class, Helen carrying their leftover cupcakes and Catherine bestowing them on passing classmates in the halls, the ones she likes. Actually, I just liked that last one's earrings, she confides as they're going into English class, I don't even know her at all.

29. Evan's play: *Twelfth Night,* he replies. I don't know why I didn't ask you earlier, Helen says, feeling sheepish. They are drinking beer on Christmas Eve with most of the lights off, after their parents have gone upstairs. Across the room, Grace has fallen asleep, hair streaming down over the side of her face and the edge of the couch, nearly touching the floor. Evan says, And what about you? I mean, are you enjoying your life here?

30. Catherine's text: *Feeling spontaneous . . . A and I are going to come down to NYC next week for New Year's . . . let's meet up?*

31. Contrition: And Helen really is sorry for being the way she's been about Alexander. But the fact remains she doesn't like him, and once she reads the text she realizes the problem hasn't gone away. She isn't going to be mean about it, isn't going to be vocal, but it doesn't change the fact that she doesn't want to see him, not at all. And this is maybe the way it will always be.

32. **Evan says, opening another beer:** Helen what could possibly be in that text message that is making you cry.

33. **Prague, wasted on Catherine:** She always says, Honestly I can't say I remember that much about it.

34. **Helen's text:** *Yes! Let's do New Year's! So happy!*

35. **Cover your ears:** In their childhood, if their parents are fighting, they go to Evan's room and Helen and Grace will sit on the floor. Then Evan climbs up on the bed and performs the argument with extraordinary flourish. He has a pair of glasses he wears to be their mother and an Oxford shirt he wears to be their father. Evan is going to be famous famous famous, says Grace, and Helen says, Now be me! When Evan is being Grace, he wears pink, and when he's being Helen, he wears a headband. If things get especially loud downstairs, he belts out pop songs at a desperate volume. If that fails they just say, Grace, cover your ears, and Grace will put her head down in Helen's lap.

36. **Their mother says (and it feels like a curse):** One day you will be married and you will see, you will see. This is how it is, couples fight, they simply do.

37. **Beginning of the terrible fight:** Evan says, while they wash the dishes after Christmas dinner, Don't take this the wrong way, Helen, but as for me I never intend to

move back in with Mom and Dad. I plan on being more self-sufficient.

38. Helen surprises herself by saying: Self-sufficiency is fictional. Everyone is in some way dependent on other people. And Evan says, When you say things like that, it only makes me want to prove you wrong.

39. Practice: Grace reactivates her membership at the Park Avenue and 23rd Street New York Health & Racquet Club. Grace does not want to go to the movies with Helen and Evan and their parents on the day after Christmas because she needs to practice. Helen and Evan go to the movies with their parents but do not speak to each other, because of the fight.

40. Practice: Evan paces around the living room doing this one monologue over and over and over and over again, always messing up in the same place and then swearing. And Helen knows the line herself actually, but she just keeps sitting there on the couch with her legs crossed, eating her bowl of cereal, not looking up.

41. Practice: She is getting to be very skillful with her latte art. (You're becoming very glib about yourself, says her father.)

42. Adjustment disorder: For paperwork purposes you know we need to say something, says the therapist her parents ask her to see before Christmas—because the meltdown seems less and less likely to resolve itself, and they are concerned. The therapist clarifies: It just means you're having an intense emotional reaction. And in a way that's just how life can be.

43. **The therapist says about Catherine:** It's okay to miss her. Why don't we just take a moment and miss her?

44. **Helen says:** I think I have significantly overshared.

45. **Their father says:** I never wanted to go to therapy myself.

46. **Their mother says:** Nor did I.

47. **Grace says:** At school they give you all the sessions you want, for free. I think it's great.

48. **Evan says:** I don't need therapy, I'm a performer and I'm perilously in touch with my own emotions; there is nothing a therapist could reveal to me that I don't know; my heart is on my sleeve.

49. **Catherine texts:** *Well I'm glad to know you're taking care of yourself, that's important.*

50. **Just you wait:** When Helen turns seventeen, Catherine calls up to say, Wear a bathing suit under your school uniform, don't forget. Helen makes some insinuation that this

sounds juvenile, but in the end she promises she will. She's on the landline, the dog is barking, and Grace is in the background saying, I need the phone, Helen, can you please get off right now? The next day after school Catherine says, Okay so did you ever know about the sprinklers? Then, with a faint and glamorous smile, Oh you'll love this, just you wait. After play rehearsal, the pair of them sit together on the bleachers until dusk settles in, until the lawn goes up, all at once, in rows of long and waving plumes. Later, out there in her bathing suit under the darkening swoop of sky, bare feet in wet grass, Helen tips her head back to watch this one particular spout reach its height and start to fall.

51. Catherine, from several sprinklers away: You're supposed to run through them, Helen, not stand there considering them. Run! Frolic!

52. New Year's Eve: Alexander says, Hey, how's it going. Catherine says, I really love your earrings—those are gorgeous.

53. Helen, drunk, later: I'm sorry Alexander, did Catherine even tell you that, I'm sorry I'm sorry I'm sorry. It's only this is the thing, I have never wanted to lose her.

54. Happy New Year: Their father says to sit here on the couch please, and so they do—Evan in his ratty Middlebury sweatshirt, not looking at Helen. He displays a careful expression of defiance. She is terrifically hungover. Their father before them is looking from one to the other and back again; he says something about new year, new leaf, let's resolve to get along here. Then Grace comes clattering from the upstairs floor of the apartment, dragging the squash racquet at her side so it thunks dully down the stairs, the thunks reverberating *thunk thunk thunk*. Can you not please, Helen snarls, head pounding. I thought you were trying to be less spiteful in the new year, Grace says, and with showy indolence drops the racquet to the floor. From the kitchen their mother says, Grace you will break that and then you'll be sorry—and Evan snorts, because for as long as any of them can remember, their mother has been telling them X is going to break and it's going to be your fault, you were careless, you were trying to make a point, and now you'll be sorry. In this moment, Helen catches Evan's eye.

55. Could I also: Helen is six and Evan is four and Grace is three, and because of the sandwiches, which Helen and Evan insist they've finished but have actually conspired to throw away, their father shuts the trash can abruptly and says, Come into the living room right now please, I want to have a talk with both of you. Interlude: a stern seminar, somewhere offstage, on the subject of how lying is wrong. Eventually, glumly, they rejoin Grace at the kitchen table, the dog nosing for crumbs around their chairs. Grace looks up from her half-eaten sandwich. She says, Dad? He says, Yes? She says, Do you think you could also talk to me in the living room? Could I also get to do that?

56. Their mother imposes herself on their terrible fight: You have always been this way, the three of you, always. Coming home after school, complaining, bickering, I mean when are you ever going to start emphasizing what's going well for you instead of what's going wrong? And Grace—silent until now, just drying the dishes, saying nothing—flares up from nowhere, slams a saucepan to the countertop. She says, Don't you think we might all ask the same of you?

57. This is the year it finally occurs to Helen to ask: What did you even say that day in the living room? This is a famous story in their family and her father always loves to tell it, but he seems for a moment lost in the question. Then he says: I think I asked her how her day was going. And she said it was going pretty well.

58. Helen, drunk, still: She seizes Catherine lovingly by the wrist and leans in close to her ear. On the television, blurry in the background, the Times Square Ball shimmers and descends. Alexander is at the bar ordering an IPA and Helen wishes they could leave without him. Take my glass of water, she murmurs to Catherine. Look at Alexander. Remember what you always used to say?

59. What she used to say, remember?: I'll throw a glass of water in his face, and that will be it, I'll be gone.

60. Consider the emphasis: Helen says, You're meant to say "crownèd," not "crowned," you know. Evan says, Of course I know, I just sometimes forget. There is no one else there, and they regard each other from either side of this impasse, and in the silence between them the espresso machine hums. Finally she says, More? But he pushes the empty cup towards her; he says, I've already had far too much.

61. Because we are your parents and we say so: Grace, age eight, starts to cry. She says, But all three of us really want popcorn. We really just want it so much. So you're just making us really sad right now. Don't you care that we're so sad because of you?

62. Moment of crisis: Catherine says, You exhaust me, and twists her arm away from Helen's fingers.

63. Three, Two, One, Happy: The new year arrives, and as it does, Helen swings at the glass of water with the back of her hand so that it spills all over the tabletop and the floor, spills into Catherine's purse, spills over her stockings and the knees of Alexander's stupid-looking pants, spills everywhere. I can't believe I came here tonight with the two of you, says Helen, rising. She says, I must be insane.

Catherine is saying, Jesus Christ, Helen, and shaking the contents of her purse out on the bar. And all around them everyone is singing, as Alexander puts his hand on the sequined back of Catherine's dress.

64. Remember: When she lets herself into her parents' apartment in the early hours of this year, still wearing her celebratory paper hat and crying freely (as she figures just goes without saying by now), she finds her father sitting up. Remember, she says from the doorway, how angry I got if you waited up for me in high school? How I felt over-supervised? Do you remember that it made me feel like I was your science experiment, and not your child? Do you remember the way I used to scream at you?

65. Her father says: Are you all right? Can I get you a drink?

66. Together: Evan packs up to go back to school. Before he leaves the two of them spend a morning in the living room running his lines. When he reaches the problem monologue, he gets up on the couch and delivers the whole thing with extraordinary flourish. Impeccable, says Helen, sitting on the floor, Except remember: always "crownèd," never "crowned." He says, Stop it, stop, I know. Then Grace from the top of the stairs, rubbing her eyes, says, Some of us were trying to sleep. Cover your ears Grace, they say together. And Grace, plodding down the stairs, almost smiles. She says, You are going to break the couch, Evan, and then you'll be sorry.

67. Going-away dinner: Their father raises his drink. He says, To me it is a delight in every way to have us all together. And he takes a quick, deep breath. Anyway, cheers. Break a leg, Evan, and we will see you at your play. Their five wine glasses, making contact, chime. Their mother drinks, looks at her napkin, back up again. She says, Evan I hope you've remembered to pack everything and did you print your ticket like I asked you to?

68. Helen's text: *I'm sorry and I don't know what to do anymore.*

69. Catherine's response:

70. Act II Scene III: "I was adored once, too."

71. Squash: You can come with me, says Grace, but I'm not going to go easy on you. I'm going to destroy you. And do you even know where your goggles are? I don't have a second pair to lend you.

72. Prague: Catherine says, One day we'll go together. They are sixteen and lying on a blanket in Catherine's backyard, eating pizza, looking at the sky, and can think of no reason such a thing would fail to come to pass. It seems certain, they have set it in motion just by saying as much. She says, From there we'll go on to Vienna and we'll listen to orchestras. We'll bring nothing more than we can fit in our backpacks. We'll walk beside the Vltava and the Danube and drink beer in cafés. We'll meet numberless men in Prague and Vienna, she says. Helen laughs. She says, Will we?

73. On his way to the 3:32 out of Penn Station: Evan stops by for a final espresso. He says, I hope to see you at the play next month, by which point I'll have "learnèd" all my lines. She starts laughing, and he says, Wait stop don't cry. She says, It's just I'm very moved and also I don't know.

74. Grace, on the couch, tells Helen: Lucky you, lucky you, you still get me for two more weeks. Do you want to watch the next episode? Move over please, move over. You are, as always, completely crowding my space.

75. Always: The air is light and sweet, a thin cloud slips quickly over the sun and keeps moving on. Everything shadows, then lightens: the backyard, the side of the house, Catherine's long, bright hair. She turns her face towards Helen's, leans it on the crook of her own bent arm. She says, We will, we will. She lets her forehead touch Helen's shoulder and says, It won't end well. They'll always miss us, always, always. They'll think of us often, and wonder how it happened like it did.

Two Pisces Emote
About the Passage of Time

— — —

Christine begins to fixate on certain turning points in her own history—what might have happened otherwise, if she'd made different choices.

Sometimes at night she wakes with a watery, stranded sensation, as if something that might have been hers is dissolving. In dreams she reaches for keys, cups, doorknobs—her hands slide through them. What if she had gone to some other college, or moved to some city other than New York? (But what, then, if she had never known Daisy?)

She knows it's useless, to give attention to what can't ever change. But it's vivid, mesmerizing, to consider other lives.

The preoccupation reaches peak futility when Christine and Daisy move from Ditmas Park to the new apartment in Bushwick. An old boyfriend lives nearby; he and Christine meet up for a drink. He mentions he is dating someone new, and Christine feels unexpectedly annihilated. It's as if something breaks open, beneath a fine seam she's been holding closed, effortfully, all her life.

She didn't think she still had feelings for him, even. Now she ruminates on: how did she lose him, what mistakes did she make here? She lies on the new IKEA couch and cries endlessly, her grief like an infection. Daisy makes tea, she sits and listens. If Christine had not responded unkindly that one time. If she had not gone away that one summer. If she did not have such a temper. Then what, then what, then what?

I think I've fucked up, Christine says, her hands over her eyes. But Daisy is gently skeptical. No way, she says. You're just going through something. She fixes a piece of Christine's hair behind her ear, and her hand is soft on the side of Christine's face. It's hard when people move on, Daisy says. But at some point you have to just pull it together.

In January Daisy gets into astrology, with zeal. She'll absorb herself with research on her laptop for hours, then emerge from her room to disclose her findings, her laptop balanced in the crook of one arm, the other reaching to switch on the tea kettle.

I think what's going on with you is the influence of your moon in Capricorn, she says one night.

Christine has been watching television in a small, bleak trance, a blanket pulled up over her head. She makes herself sit upright in her cocoon. Moon in Capricorn feels very alone in the world, Daisy is explaining from the kitchen. I keep coming across the word *orphaned*.

And I have that? says Christine. Daisy is taking mugs down from the cupboard, her arm stretched up to reach the highest shelf. The tea kettle is beginning to steam, frantically.

Yes, says Daisy, That is what you have.

By February they've unpacked most of their boxes. They each turn twenty-seven—Daisy first, then Christine. On the morning of her birthday, before work, in their kitchen, Christine makes coffee and tries to explain how, for the first time ever, she is experiencing her age as a problem, a sort of mismatch. I feel too messy to be twenty-seven, she says. Twenty-seven should feel clearer. I haven't achieved it. For one thing, I'm a receptionist. A *temp* receptionist.

Outside their window, it's starting to rain. Inside the light casts both their faces in a warm glow. Have a little perspective, says Daisy, who has a better job, at a startup, writing marketing copy. She says, It could be worse: I've been twenty-seven for days now. Christine makes a show of frowning as she pours herself some coffee. It's a joke, Daisy says. Come on—it's funny! Can you pour me a cup?

That weekend they throw a shared birthday party. Daisy emails the invitation with the subject *Two Pisces Emote About the Passage of Time*. They both find that extremely clever, but the party is only okay. Christine drinks several cocktails too quickly, becomes ensnared in conversation with a co-worker of Daisy's. They talk about a movie Christine loves, and he tells her that it's overrated—Not that I've seen it, he adds, but from everything I've heard. Later, someone by the bar puts a hand on the small of Christine's back to move her aside as he passes, a gesture so proprietary that Christine has to excuse herself, seething, to smoke a cigarette outside. Men think they can just move us out of the way, she says to the girl who gives her a light out on the sidewalk, and though she has offered no context, the girl says: For real.

I always forget I mostly hate this bar, Christine says later, while she and Daisy stand in line for the bathroom. Daisy leans her head against Christine's shoulder and says, What we like is the idea of it.

For a birthday gift, Daisy buys Christine an astrological reading, to be conducted by video chat. Christine sets it up for the following Tuesday night—she emails the date, time, and place of her birth in advance. The astrologer, ethereal yet severe in the blurry chat window, explains that Christine's natal chart shows a complex gathering of planets in her Twelfth House of Self-Undoing.

Also, he says, her Mars placement makes her impulsive, direct, and prone to irritation. It's important you find healthy avenues for aggression, the astrologer tells her, as if he were prescribing a vitamin. You might take up martial arts, he says.

Impulsively, Christine does. She signs up for a class at the gym, and actually she finds she does love it, loves to punch and smack and kick, loves the way her leg flares out to meet the impassive bulk of the punching bag. Sweaty, shaking her hair out of her eyes, she feels exquisite, powerful, nearly divine. She goes back every week. She begins to feel better.

You are a goddess of war, says Daisy, who sometimes comes along to the gym, to use the bouldering wall. She reports that whenever she stops for a drink of water, she can see Christine in action through the glass door to the kickboxing room. Later, after her class, Christine will always join Daisy at the bouldering wall, and the two of them stand before its warty, multicolor grips, chalking their hands while Daisy points out ascents she expects Christine can handle.

Daisy is experienced at this, whereas Christine has almost no technique. She enjoys it, though: the trial-and-error climb, and then the controlled fall from the top, like she is a cat dropping out of a tree. Also she finds it hypnotic to sit and watch Daisy—balletic and agile, her shoulders bare in her tank top, her hair in a braid down her back. You're gorgeous up there, Christine tells her admiringly, one night after Daisy finishes a climb and is wiping chalk from her hands.

Daisy responds, grandly, I'm gorgeous everywhere. She twirls then, she kicks over her water bottle, so then they have to run to the locker room for paper towels. I'm an idiot, says Daisy on her hands and knees, sopping up water, laughing.

Afterward they wash their hands, side by side at the locker-room sink. Daisy cups her palms, splashes water over her face. Then she meets Christine's eyes in the mirror, water running down her cheekbones and neck.

Okay, Daisy says. Can I tell you something?

• • •

And this is what unnerves Christine: the unseen potential in people she trusts. Lurking injury, how anyone could hurt her, leave her, any moment. Lately she's been waking up at night, gripped with a steep and breathless dread. Other times she dreams she is married to someone wonderful, but then she's knocking on their door and he won't open it. He keeps coming to the window, but when he sees it's her, he lets the curtain subside, placidly, back over his face. He looks resigned, though each time she knocks, he returns again to the window. It's as if he's hopeful someone is coming who isn't her.

She dreams this, too: Daisy walks through the apartment refusing to acknowledge Christine. Not in an angry way, exactly, only with the discipline of someone who has made the best decision, the clear and necessary choice. She looks, maybe, a little smug. Eventually she has Christine's room removed, physically, from the apartment, sliced away as if it were an enormous square of cake. Afterward they stand together in the kitchen, and when Daisy finally speaks, her tone is relieved: I didn't anticipate missing you, she says. And as it turns out, I don't.

On this night after Daisy says, at the gym, that she's moving to Austin, Christine describes the dream in detail, aware she is trying to seem maximally vulnerable and pained. It's a terrible dream, she says. It makes me feel alone.

Maybe she can convince Daisy not to do it. They've decamped from the gym to a nearby bar, somewhere they can have a beer and talk this over, as Daisy put it. Daisy is quick to tell Christine that sharing the dream is a low blow—utterly low and unfair to disclose in this particular conversation. She says, You want me to feel worse than I already do.

Fine, says Christine hotly, Forgive me. She gestures to the bartender, *another*. She feels like a skipping record: We only *just* moved, she keeps saying, inanely. But Daisy is patient. I know, she says. It's just that the job came up and I want the job.

It wasn't intentional, Daisy says. Surely you can understand that.

At the end of March they break their lease. Daisy is the one who takes the couch, because Christine has not yet paid her back for it.

Christine rents a studio—before this, she has never lived alone. The little couch she buys is delivered to the first floor, deposited in a cardboard box by the stairs. Afterward, she is unable to arrive at a satisfactory explanation of how she moved it to the third floor on her own. I guess I sort of rolled it end over end, she says to Daisy on the phone, I must have. The memory is vague. Daisy laughs and says, Did you black out or something?

The studio looks out on the backs of other buildings. In April, Christine tries growing plants on the fire escape— but then there is a strange, late snowfall, and in the middle of the night she has to bring them all in and set them by the radiator as the little cones of snow melt down. I'm sorry, she says to the plants, I didn't foresee this.

It isn't quiet, her new neighborhood. But somehow it's like her apartment is hermetically sealed, hushed and silent as a small church. Sometimes this is serene and reminds her of childhood, of unearthing certain pleasures of solitude, lying across her bed, lost in thought. Other times the isolation of the apartment is an experience of disorientation and strange grief. Having watched Daisy box up her life and let go of what she would not be bringing with her, Christine decides to clear out many of her own belongings. She appreciates the sensation of stripping away what once delighted her—a feeling like she is getting out ahead of the inevitable. She bags clothes and sets them by the door, and the silence of her apartment seems to divorce her from context. She could be any person, anywhere.

Daisy texts, *When are you visiting? Will it be soon?* But something is shifting. *I can't come*, Christine tells her. *I have to stay here.*

She says it because something in New York is beginning to obsess her—she feels a small, troubling dissolution around her own sense of belonging, a feeling like she's watching over an animal that could run from her. She has to stay close. In the silence of the apartment, she feels like she is drifting with the tide, and she tells herself out loud: You live here. And she thinks of Daisy's astrologer who said: This is a watery phase of your life. You'll feel like you're going in circles. The current is taking you where you can't see. As a child she moved frequently, it's something she's always been proud of, it makes her feel unusual, interesting, special. Daisy has always been jealous: All I have is Ohio, she likes to say.

Now the question of home transfixes Christine.

New York is the only city she's lived in for more than five years. It's where she first became alert to the pleasures of knowing a place. Sometimes she cannot fathom Daisy's choice to go, it seems to her like severing an artery. New York has symbolic weight for me, she says one night on the phone—and it feels, to her relief, like she has finally found words to describe all this. But Daisy only laughs at her: New York has symbolic weight for everyone, she says, I hate to break it to you. Later, she sends Christine a photo of herself, wearing a short-sleeve T-shirt, eating tacos in the sun.

But Christine means something different, about the accrual of personal history. About what it is to walk through this city and feel stirrings of meaning arise in places she has been. She misses the feeling of knowing her friend is in the next room, or will be home later. She liked feeling seen in this daily way by someone, in the course of years. With Daisy gone, she finds her ideas about home and where she might locate it flower out disturbingly. When she's alone, images come to her unbidden of living in all kinds of places—at the beach, in other countries, closer to her family, alone in a new city. The more ideas she has, the more possibilities she conjures, the more tenuous and unlikely home seems.

She finds her heart racing on subway platforms, or on weekend mornings waking up. She dreams she is living in an empty, quiet cube that has no door.

One day on the street, in May, the city becoming warm and living again, someone thinks he knows her, he pursues her up the block. I'm sorry, she tells him, turning at the corner when he touches her shoulder, I don't think we've met—and then she is irritated to feel her eyes well up with tears. I'm so sorry I chased you, says the man, obviously mortified. I didn't mean to upset you. I feel terrible. He runs a hand through his hair, he emanates concern.

No, this isn't your fault, Christine is saying, wiping her eyes with the heel of her palm. No, I'm sorry, my friend moved. It's hard to explain.

She tips her head back, and the pattern of clouds blurs and shifts like wet ink. Traffic grumbles in her ears. Let me get you a coffee or something, she hears this man saying to her, apologetic. I'm Luke. Could I do that for you?

Later Daisy will ask what even possessed her to agree. Very unlike you, she says, Though don't get me wrong, I'm delighted. She adds, But please don't ever marry him: Christine McQueen, what a terrible rhyme. I won't be able to take you seriously. They both start laughing and then they can't stop. I'm honestly having trouble breathing, Christine says into the phone. Daisy is cooking something in the background, her dishes clatter in Christine's ear.

Then something shifts again.

She starts to find the weight of memory in the city oppresses her, infiltrates her present moment. Kissing Luke good night outside a bar, she realizes she once kissed someone else over there on the opposite side of 7th Avenue. Meeting a college friend for a drink at a new place in her neighborhood, she realizes she's been here before, only now the bar has a different name, has multicolored lights strung up, license plates nailed into the wall, an imitation of a place that's been here longer.

My friend lives *there*, she says too emphatically to the bartender, pointing at Texas above the beer taps, and he laughs at her a little cruelly. When the city starts to bleed meaning this way, it feels like a sequence in a movie, though she can't precisely say how so. She feels like she is having an experience she knew would come to pass, as if she has traveled back to herself in these specific years in an attempt to change something immutable in her fate. She tries describing this to Daisy on the phone, but Daisy just keeps asking which movie she means. Not one particular movie, says Christine. I'm saying *like* a movie, you're not hearing me.

She begins to consider how it would be to actually move away, a small experiment in self-betrayal. Home is deserting me, she tells someone at work, making coffee in the break room. She surprises herself by saying it, a very personal disclosure.

Sometimes she resurfaces from the subway onto some familiar corner, or the light hits the side of a particular building—and then she feels disbelief that the city existed before her and will without her. In books it always supplies a small thrill when a place of some private meaning is invoked: Washington Square Park, Amsterdam Avenue, the bar on Greenwich Avenue. The Cooper Hewitt, the corner of 19th and Irving, West 12th Street. She writes exclamation marks in the margins, saves the moments of significance, intersections with her own existence. Other times it feels like she's living in a kind of dreamscape where imaginary futures hover everywhere, mapped onto different points around the city: detailed, fading, insubstantial. Any time she's in Bushwick—running an errand, or meeting a friend—she tends to imagine the years she and Daisy would have shared on Stanhope Street. She walks past the building and she'll picture them inside: Daisy making tea, or Daisy saying, Calm down, don't lose your temper with me, I'm listening.

So on the few occasions Daisy is seized by moods of regret, Christine takes a perverse pleasure in it. She likes them both suffering the same lost vision. One night Daisy calls in the middle of the night. I miss you, she says. I feel fucking stupid, I don't know where I am sometimes. Christine turns on the light. She says, You'll be okay.

When she thinks about childhood, about the games she would play, imagining herself grown up, she can hardly believe she is still living on that same continuous timeline. In bars on weekends, she and Luke and their friends discuss their place in the larger unraveling of everything. They discuss the person they can't imagine will be elected in the fall, and should they have children in the face of looming climate catastrophe. The future feels like it is coming fast, like it will be terrifying. She considers how Luke is genuinely reliable—he would surely protect their hypothetical family in the inevitable event of environmental apocalypse, for example, and sometimes this seems like the clearest reason for being with him. He is a gentler person than she is, fundamentally: I don't take anyone's shit, she says to him in passing one night at his apartment, and though she's talking about someone else, a co-worker who condescended to her in a meeting, Luke seems to recoil as if she is dangerous.

In a newspaper obituary around this time, she reads the sentence "She did not suffer fools," and it is in an aspirational spirit that she writes it down and tapes it to her mirror. She remembers the astrologer highlighting her Mars in Aries: the wild unleashing thrill of adrenaline, any time she allows herself to say something cutting, to storm away. One night in June she fights with Luke while they're cooking at her apartment, she slams out into the street, into the humid dark night, and when he doesn't follow her she walks miles through Brooklyn. She has no keys, no wallet with her—I have nothing, she wants to say to someone.

That's a bit much, she can picture Daisy saying. I'm just one person who left. Your life is pretty good. She starts to have dreams of Daisy saying this, dreams where Christine tries to hit her but her hands are too heavy to lift. She wakes up mortified to have lost her temper, as if it really happened. Meanwhile in her waking life, she repeatedly loses her temper with Luke. It embarrasses her in the aftermath, it always does, her reactions looming out of proportion—her words heedless, unforgiving, and appalling when reviewed. She'd like to take things not so personally. Though Daisy has always adored her temper: It lights me up, she likes to say. It's who you are.

Then it's July, hot and damp. One night, Christine argues with Luke in a restaurant, and when she gets up and says she's leaving, he lets her, as if defusing the tension is the thing that matters most. She can feel his eyes follow her out the door into the fine rain. Waiting for the light to change at 6th, she feels irritable and grim, disturbed and broken, and when a taxi blares its horn she says aloud to no one: Fuck you.

As if to punish her, the rain picks up with huge and ominous momentum. The light changes, headlights illuminate bright swaths in wet pavement. She crosses the street at a run and takes shelter under the awning of a closed bagel shop to root for her umbrella in her bag. When she realizes she's left it in the restaurant, she tips her head back against the glass storefront, closes her eyes.

The sound of the cascading storm is a long, unceasing hiss on the pavement.

Then a man and woman flail breathlessly into the space beside her, laughing helplessly. Christine opens her eyes, looks over to smile weakly in greeting, but they seem to barely register her. Oh my god, the woman is saying mirthfully, as she wipes her face with her hands, pushes them back through her wet hair like she is stepping from a shower. An expression of longing passes over the man's face, and he reaches out and kisses her, and in Christine's chest something desperate seems to unfurl.

It has been three months since Daisy moved. Through this first sad flush of their apartness, Christine has been unable to comprehend why other people's happiness provokes her greatest longing for her friend. Daisy might smirk, if she were here—clocking the look on Christine's face. She'd say to this couple, Excuse me, no displays of affection in front of my sad friend. Or she might turn to Christine with a parody of infatuation on her face and say, Should we also kiss? Probably we should, right? This is when the sound escapes from Christine, a wail that surprises her as much as it seems to surprise the other two. They turn to look at her with alarm. They will tell this story for years, Christine thinks. Probably they will laugh, recalling the overreacting girl in the rainstorm. And this inevitability fills her with such anger that when the couple asks, Are you all right? Christine steps into the torrent and doesn't look back.

The city is a shiny, dissolving stain before her, it wavers in her vision. As she walks, she reaches into her pocket and dials Daisy, rain beading furiously on the screen of her phone, the drops clinging to each other. She presses send on the call, she hears the tiny ring and then the crackle of the line, a small opening in time and space. The phone is slick in her hand, as Daisy's miniature voice in the storm says, Chris? Hello?

Just then the phone is falling from her grasp. It slips into a rivulet of water, a clear splotch of light, and goes streaming toward the storm drain. Christine gets on her knees; she's like a child in a tide pool. Her hands are like two starfish in the water. The man and woman from the awning float above with their umbrella saying, Let us help you, tell us what you lost. The M8 bus is going past her, and the water rising from its wheels is bright abundant champagne gold. The rain is sliding down her face and neck, the phone keeps slipping from her fingers, the phone becomes a fish that swims away. The bus is disappearing toward the Hudson, but when Christine looks back here comes the same M8. Same graffiti swirled across its front, and so much tidal water rising up again. She is a skipping record. She is the phases of the moon. She is a city bus forever circling this route, as Daisy's voice, below the water, tries to say her name.

Moments Earlier

—— —— ——

Kelly lands in a heap when she falls down the stairs—she falls half a flight at least, hits the entryway tile.

Daniel says he can't remember screaming. Owen tells him that he did scream, a shout that echoed in the stairwell.

Owen, for his part, keeps his cool—he always tries to be the sort of person who can do this, remain composed, unflappable. The kind of person who would coolly say to Kelly, in the hours after she flew back from Greece, in the moments before she fell down his stairs, Do you think posting so many photos affected your ability to actually *experience* Athens? Didn't you feel not entirely present? Is it okay to ask you that?

Ask me anything, Kelly told him—affectionate but also like *try me*. She sipped water from a coffee mug (it was all they'd had to offer her) and leaned against the fridge, her suitcase in the corner. Daniel was looking for his wallet. Owen was picturing a photo he'd seen on the internet: Kelly at the Parthenon, arms thrown wide in sheer delight. On the fridge behind her, postcards she'd sent them were taped up next to Daniel's teaching schedule, plus a photo from college at an off-campus bar, Erin and Kelly's shared birthday party, the four of them all drunk and hugging.

Kelly put down the mug and started putting on her lipstick. She said, Will Erin be extremely mad we're late? Owen said, No question, and Kelly laughed and said, Oh well, I'll text her. Daniel ran his hands through his hair—he needed a haircut, in Owen's opinion. Did I have my wallet when we left the laundromat? Daniel was saying, and he started lifting up the couch cushions. Owen said, I can't remember, sorry, and then he said to Kelly, What?

Nothing, Kelly told him, with this look on her face. Just, I'm glad to be here. Owen felt restless then; he stuffed his hands into his pockets. Hey Daniel? he said. Listen, I'll spot you, we're really very late.

It was unkind, what he said about her photos—that's what Owen remembers thinking as they went into the hall, as they went down the stairs. He regretted having said it, he felt suddenly queasy. He decided that later, he'd say he was sorry. They were on their way to meet Erin downtown. The four of them would have a drink, they would trade strong opinions about where to go to dinner, this was the plan: a reunion. All week Kelly had been emailing, *Can't wait :)* and, *How has it been six whole months!* and *See you very very soon,* etc.

Then Kelly fell. Then Daniel screamed. Now Owen is calling an ambulance, looking down at Daniel bent across her, Daniel telling her, Don't worry you'll be fine. Can she even hear him? The dispatcher says to Owen, Sir, it's critical she doesn't move. But it doesn't seem to him she could; she's lying very still. Daniel's frantic, his fingers pressed to Kelly's wrist, her neck. Age, says the dispatcher, and Owen says, Um, um, twenty-two?

The EMTs arrive, they say Owen and Daniel should come to the hospital. They say "cardiac episode," though Owen thought she only lost her footing when, below him on the stairs, she dropped away. Instinctively he'd reached for her, succeeded in catching briefly at the shoulder of her coat. Afterward, nonsensically, he keeps thinking: *almost.* From the hospital waiting room, pressing his forehead to the glass of a window, watching car headlights swim past below, he calls Erin. She picks up, annoyed. Are you just ignoring my texts? This is late even by your standards. And he tells her. Wait, she says. Wait please slow down. He says, Come here, you need to come here. We called her parents—they're getting on a plane, somehow, I mean they're coming.

Erin shows up at the waiting room thirty minutes later, still dressed for dinner—heels, blazer. Oh no, she says. Look at you, both of you. Daniel starts crying. Owen says, Um so, they're telling us brain damage, maybe her brain is damaged. Not from the fall, but from this cardiac episode, from loss of air to, well, but they say that there's no way to know until she wakes up. Erin is taking off her scarf. She says, But then falling down the stairs, what about that? Owen says, We don't know, they don't know. They've got her in this coma—induced, no, maintained—they're watching her. They have her in a kind of cooling bed, and they said it's what you do, um, when you're worried about a brain, because scientifically, it's that near-victims of drowning, they I guess have better outcomes when it happens in cold water.

Daniel takes a wavering breath, he fiddles with the zipper on his jacket. He says, She'll be in that for twelve hours, in this deep freeze, then they'll bring her out of it, and then. Owen says, No actually, not a deep freeze. Not freezing: cooling. Daniel says, Oh, true, that may be the wrong term, and he scratches vaguely at his ear as Owen says, It is, yeah, it's wrong.

Erin presses both her hands together, draws them to her throat. Okay, she says, Well, we can't think about this, not until we know more. Right? Owen sees a flicker of panic move across her face, but then she gives them each a perfunctory hug and says, Have you eaten? I haven't eaten. And she goes and buys three bags of cheesy popcorn from the snack machines across the room. So they end up in blue vinyl chairs, quiet, chewing, their fingers accumulating pale cheese film. Erin brushes crumbs from her coat, her hands sort of shaking. She says, I'm trying to understand, could fright in the moment of falling lead to a cardiac incident? Or would it only ever be cardiac incident first? Owen says, It must be genetic, her grandmother, remember that story? Daniel has his head down on his knees, has laced his fingers over the back of his neck. Then Erin says, Think of the odds. After all those months traveling, of all places she's standing on your stairs. But Daniel lifts his head and says: I don't think we should pursue this kind of thinking, I don't feel that we should do that.

Then comes another call from Kelly's parents, and Owen unfolds out of his chair, pacing in front of Daniel and Erin, nodding and nodding his head, feeling himself becoming glazed and disoriented. Her parents are getting on a plane from LAX to JFK. An aunt who lives in Brooklyn is on her way to the hospital. This aunt has Owen's phone number, as does Kelly's brother who will stay in California, and Owen should keep these two updated while her parents are in flight.

I will, I will, he tells them, but then can't find what to say next so he lets Erin take the phone. Daniel pats the chair beside him, Owen sits. Erin says to Kelly's father, The three of us are here, Daniel and Owen and me, and when you get here, we will be here, I promise, and we'll find your sister, too. Erin hangs up; she frowns, gives a brief twist of her head like an animal shaking off water. She says in a very small voice, Now they have to shut off their phones. Can you imagine?

A feeling of confinement comes over Owen then, stealthy and crushing—he'd like to be out of this room, be somewhere else, alone. But Daniel beats him to it: running his hands through his hair again, bringing them down over his temples, looking from Owen to Erin, Erin to Owen. He says, I maybe just need to go for a walk. I think I have to walk around, would that be okay? He bounces a little on the balls of his feet. He's always had this instinct, this nervous energy. It gets under Owen's skin, it always has. Studying, in college, Daniel would pace the hallways of their freshman dorm, habitually roving, French vocabulary flash cards in hand. Murmuring Je voudrais un café and whatever, intermittently appearing in the open doorways to the room that Daniel shared with Owen and, across the hall, the one that Erin shared with Kelly.

They would listen to his approach, his muttered French verb conjugations, then listen to him fade away. Whereas Erin did her homework in the library—usually in the precise amount of time she'd allotted to complete it—and

Owen might go hours without moving from the place on his bed where he liked to sit and read, his back against the cinder block wall. Kelly, for her part, sat on the floor, her novels and notes spread around her. With both their doors propped open, Owen could see Kelly from where he sat, and they'd wave at each other, a well-worn joke. She had to shield her eyes at certain times of day to see him, because of the way the light came in behind him through the window. That, she said once, plus your general personal radiance, and Owen rolled his eyes.

Now, he says abruptly, to Daniel and to Erin, Do you know, earlier tonight, I was criticizing her social media feed? I mean what the fuck is honestly actually wrong with me? He stands suddenly, as Daniel looks away and balls his fists, but Erin says, with an adamant, desperate waving of both hands, No, stop. Because maybe she is going to be fine, so you don't have to, like, let's not. Okay?

She looks from one of them to the other. Daniel says, Look I can't sit here like this. I'm going to go. I'm going to go walk around. He gets up, the sliding doors part for him as he leaves. Erin watches him until the doors seal up behind him, and then she looks back at Owen, sort of dazed, as if she's only now remembering she knows him.

What story? Erin says, and it takes him a moment to realize what she's asking. Oh, he says, Kelly's grandmother, you remember. But Erin only looks at him. I never heard it, she says, I don't know what you mean.

Years earlier, when Kelly told Owen this story, she was writing about it for freshman comp, a required course. The two of them were in the same section, Tuesdays and Thursdays at noon. The *horror*, he remembered Kelly would say darkly, anytime someone mentioned the class, which both of them detested. All semester she would cross the hall to lean against his doorway and read, with indignant relish, the most extremely boring sections of the Academic Writing textbook. *Today we'll look at strategies for comprehending what you've read!* he remembered her intoning. *Remember to stop after each section and check that you have really understood.* Then she'd flutter the pages of that week's reading and say, Can you believe they get to *make* us do this? It made Owen jumpy and impatient, the way Kelly liked to talk. The way she sometimes said things, just to hear the way they sounded. Look, he said, I hate the class, but yes it is credible to me we're required to take it. Kelly exhaled; she covered her face with the book. She said, But Owen I can't do it. I just can't. Owen said, You have to, though, I mean you'll have to, is the thing.

One week they were assigned to write on the subject of family. It was the only assignment of serious interest to either of them. My grandmother died very young, Kelly told him, her voice unusually measured. She was sitting on his floor in a white square of sunlight, her back against Daniel's desk. She'd lost her computer charger somewhere on campus, it could not be recovered, so if Erin was out then Kelly would cross the hall to charge off one of theirs. She said, I'm writing about this more from an imaginative position, like what would have happened if she'd lived, how life might have been different than it was. Because I did think that was interesting, what the TA said—about how it can be just as truthful to tell what might have happened, as it is to tell what did. More so, maybe, even. I mean I know you don't like that TA, but.

Branches shifted in the window, their shadows moved along the floor, and from somewhere out on the quad a strange noise rose up. Owen couldn't identify it, but right away it faded. He wasn't sure what to say, so he asked her, Which grandmother? Oh, Kelly said, My father's mother. My father was six, and if you can believe this, he was in the car. My grandmother drove their car off the road, and she died. But my father was fine. Of course, it was 1965, there was no autopsy, they'll never know the reason. And there are times I've asked my father, don't you want to figure out what happened here? But he says no. I think, you know, he feels he shouldn't be affected, because all this time has passed. I mean this happened to my father when he was six, but here he is always saying: My *sister* has had a very hard life. My sister lost her mother at the age of *two*.

Kelly seemed to take interest in the tops of her knees then, which were bent to her chest. It must have been spring, the window behind her was open. Owen said, That's really, I mean, and clicked his pen a few times over. Kelly looked up; he was sitting there with a draft of his essay open on his lap. She said, My father doesn't know that it's okay to grieve for things that might have been. Anyway, what about you though? Are you still writing yours about your cat?

He felt uneasy, he had an impulse to sit next to her. He said, Uh, now I'm not. Now that idea is sounding really kind of stupid. Thanks for coming over here, and taking our electricity, and putting things in horrible perspective.

Kelly laughed as she reached to unplug her laptop. He thought she was going to say more, but instead they both heard Daniel intoning vocabulary down the hall—La gare, le billet, se dépêcher—and maybe those were Erin's foot-steps on the stairs. Owen looked out the window; in the wind the branches moved like waves. Anyway, Kelly was saying, Thanks for the charge. I think this will be enough to tide me over. Then Erin came around the corner—she was standing in his doorway, alert, her smile fading. She seemed to react to something in the air. What did she see in both their faces to make her ask: What happened here?

· · ·

In the years after the night Kelly falls down the stairs, only Erin keeps on living in New York. I like my job so much, she insists to Owen. So I'm fine.

Daniel moves to Utah. He seems to feel the same as Owen, like he needs to make a change. He starts teaching high school French and—he tells Erin, who tells Owen—he takes up hiking in a serious way, he just wants to walk and walk.

Owen relocates to DC. He takes this internship, then a PR job that turns out to be okay. He gets into yoga, indoor rock-climbing, half-marathons; he goes running for miles along the Potomac. Then one day, when he's been living there a couple years, he takes out his phone and starts reading, compulsively, his whole email history with Kelly.

Well I bet that's pretty normal, Erin tells him. They try to catch up when they can on the phone. He gets bad cell reception at his place, so he sits on the building's front stoop while they talk, as people go past him running, or on bicycles, with strollers and dogs, in fading light.

I think I disagree, Owen tells her. It doesn't feel normal. I'm not so sure it's healthy. He tells Erin it's unplanned, it just happens, but often: waiting for toast in the morning, or just having taken a shower, or walking from the elevator to his desk. He'll just search Kelly's name in his phone and start perusing, lose all track of time, the toast gone cold, work emails unopened, whatever. It feels out of my control, he tells Erin. It makes me feel crazy. But she insists, Well, no, I'm certain that it's normal, and he can hear the New York street noise in the background: clamorous voices, the growl of traffic, an MTA announcement as Erin descends into a subway station. She seems only to call him when she's walking from one place to another.

For several months that year Owen dates this med student, Natalie. He likes her; so why does he go and tell her everything in so much detail? I've heard of it, Natalie says when he blurts some of this out one night over dinner at her apartment—he's brought wine, she made pasta. Congenital, Natalie says. Usually, there's family history, right?

He says, I have always felt guilty, to be honest. I was the one behind her on the stairs. Later, I found out I was the only one of us who knew this thing about her grandmother. Not that it changes anything, but. I always felt sort of responsible for her—well no that's not the word. I felt, I don't know what I felt. I'm sorry, do you want another glass? Natalie says, Yes, sure, I'll have another. She reaches to take his hand, but it only makes him feel restless, and he wonders should he change the subject. The next day he tries deleting some emails, an effort to be present, stop dwelling, but then he arrives at this one that he really likes, with its total exuberance—*Hello look at this photo, isn't Sweden*

BEAUTIFUL, I'm never leaving—and he decides he won't delete them, after all.

In the months when he was first receiving Kelly's emails, they had just graduated from college, and she had begun her trip through Europe. The rest of them were brand-new transplants to New York—he and Daniel rented a U-Haul in June to move their things together, and in September, Erin followed, started coding software for a startup whose cutesy name Daniel and Owen mocked gently behind her back. Daniel was in his first semester of a PhD in French. Owen was tutoring, to supplement, in theory, freelance writing. And Kelly was sending them all these triple-cc'd emails, Hello from Copenhagen, Normandy, Berlin, etc., and mailing them postcards they taped to the fridge. All of this is strange now to remember. Owen and Daniel shared a one-bedroom far uptown, so Owen would email her back from his futon bed in the living room, laptop open on his stomach, while Daniel paced a short loop from the front door into his room and back again, making notes in the margins of books or grading quizzes.

Owen wrote, *You will be glad to know the change in location has changed Daniel not at all.* Kelly wrote back, *Sigh of relief!* She added, *Stop being so gloomy in your emails, you can stop hinting how it's going to be. Europe is beautiful, everyone I meet is wonderful. Let me have this before I join you in a lifetime of English-major underemployment.*

I'm totally realistic about my prospects and expect to spend my life inhabiting a series of increasingly expensive couches belonging to Erin. You can tell her I said so, xox.

When he read this aloud off his phone, at the bar they always liked on Greenwich Avenue, Erin laughed and put her hands over her face. Daniel polished off his beer and said, Too true, Erin makes so much more money than any of us. She elbowed him, he pretended to be injured. It was November, and Kelly was in Dublin. Her latest email described Trinity College, a pub she frequented, and a bridge over the Liffey she particularly liked. Owen said, I miss her, but it didn't seem like either of them heard him. Erin was finishing her drink, Daniel waving down the bartender, joking that Erin would have to pay for the next round, seeing as she could afford it.

Outside, an early snow was falling thinly on the sidewalks. Owen had not expected to feel Kelly's absence on nights like this: the three of them without her in New York. When she first announced her plan to go away and travel, over Chinese takeout senior year, it had been a curious, small relief, and Owen left the feeling unexamined. Instead he'd stirred his noodles in their paper takeout box and listened to her chat, rhapsodic, about the profound and ancient beauty of the Greek language. All through college he would have said there was this space between him and Kelly—so much of what she said to him seemed inexcusably frivolous. Proust, she once told him appreciatively, from across a table in the library, just knows how to write such a beautiful sentence. She thumbed at the pages; they made a zippering sound on her skin. He stayed quiet and did not suggest that this was no observation of staggering insight.

That was senior year, back when the four of them could spend whole Sundays around a table in the library, a little hungover from whatever party they'd been at the night before. He still recalls one morning, cold and bright, Kelly lifting her sunglasses away from her face on the library steps. I just want to be enthusiastic and express how I love library Sundays, she said. I love them with abandon. I wish they didn't have to end in May. Owen, freezing, hugged his coat closer. He said, Sure, agreed. Are we going inside? Another time, at an after-party for a play that Kelly starred in, he recalled her dancing across the room to the place where he was leaning, ill at ease, against the wall. I'm having so much *fun*, she said, and he was possessed by a bottled feeling, like this moment was passing him by; he could not find the words to answer her.

He wished he understood her better, he wanted to. He and Daniel were a solid match, the kind of roommates who could pass hours in the dorm in easy silence. Owen liked the way, if they ran into each other in another part of campus, Daniel brightened visibly. Then Erin was this intent, productive presence—she had, Daniel said once, an actually terrifying administrative drive. She would come home from class, from jazz ensemble, from her internship, she'd put down her bag and propose they all go to dinner now, or they should come with her to X lecture or Y film screening tonight, it was going to be excellent. Erin was the one who'd molded them all into a shabby, sudden whole, appearing in their doorway hours after move-in freshman year to ask would they like to go with her and her delightful new roommate to the ice-cream social? Her dark hair was pulled back from her face, the roommate behind her wore a yellow shirt. They had honestly been thinking they might not even go, it sounded stupid, but Daniel said, Why not, we'll come along. Owen remembered Kelly, the invoked roommate, sort of in the background, smiling openly.

Of course he always cared for her, it was just that something changed—once Kelly was traveling he depended on her emails in a way Daniel and Erin seemed not too. Well sure, Erin tells him on one of their phone calls, and in the background a car honks, someone starts shouting. Erin says, I mean that much was clear. And so what? So you were always hard on her. Like what can you do? Be kinder to yourself. Of late, Owen's mostly been reading and rereading one email from Kelly's first week away: *Dear O, Hi from Paris! Hard to believe you've now written back a third time. Don't take this the wrong way, but it's thrilling to see you break character. I'm flattered, though should note we're in danger of establishing a healthy pattern here.*

What did I do to provoke this—or does it have nothing to do with me? Is real life agreeing with you, softening your edges? Or is real life just the worst, and you're pining for the past?

He remembered lying on his back on the futon, as he read it for the first time. Daniel was at the kitchen counter eating cereal, formulating a shared grocery list aloud, paying no attention to Owen, whose cursor blinked feverishly in the corner of a fresh email, *re: What have you done with Owen.* Daniel was saying they were out of paper towels— Oh and orange juice, he said. Is that it? Anything else you need? Owen?

No, he said, Nothing, totally set, thanks. To Kelly, he typed: *Dearest K, No comment.*

All these things he says to Natalie in these months—over the course of so many dinners at her place, breakfasts at his, long runs together, and movie dates, and drinks in bars—it feels good to tell her, a kind of offloading sensation that both frightens and relieves him. Like something opens in his chest and the contents slide away. How after Kelly fell, after the hospital, after the funeral and everything, Owen and Daniel had arguments, raging fights about nothing: unwashed dishes, expired whatever in the fridge. How it had never been that way with them, how they started going crazy over old things from college, stuff they'd never talked about, things that hadn't seemed to matter at the time. How Daniel started staying at his office later and later, even sleeping there some nights. How when their lease was up they said it might improve things if they lived apart. How Owen made the excuse that he was sick of the futon—he said a year was about as much as he could do, living that way. They moved out, Daniel went home to his parents' in Boston, saying it would just be for the summer and he'd see them in the fall. And Owen lived on Erin's couch for those three months. We drank way too much, he tells Natalie, who looks troubled but puts her hand on his. He says, Just me and Erin at home, or we'd go walking blocks and blocks around New York at night. It was terrible, we didn't know what to do with ourselves, we were always crying. I remember Erin would say, We can't think about it, we just have to find things to do with our time. She called Daniel almost every day, but I never did. She'd sit on the fire escape and talk with the window closed. And then instead of coming back to the city Daniel takes this high school teaching job, he tells us he's going on leave from the PhD. He says he just has to process things alone, he'll just do this for one year and he'll be back, he promises. He came to the city once more before he moved out West, I think it was August, the three of us had a drink. Margaritas, on some rooftop, awful. We tried to talk about her, about what happened, but it was like, I don't know. I remember Erin said, Okay enough, let's get the check, I can't, I want to go home. I remember hugging Daniel, I said, Good luck and let us know how you are there, and he said, Definitely I will. But actually we don't keep up at all, it's only Erin who's in touch with him, and rarely, to be honest.

The night he says all this to Natalie, they're walking to a restaurant for dinner. They meet up when she finishes class, and she comes out of the front door buttoning her jacket, putting papers in her bag. She kisses him hello, her hand on the side of his face, and they go for a drink at a bar down the block, catch up about her day. Then she is talking about anatomy lab, the cardiovascular system, its intricacies, and out of nowhere he is saying all of this. Let's walk, Natalie says, let's walk to dinner. She grasps his arm and then lets go. The light is all but faded as they come to Dupont Circle, the windows have a dusky shine, cars in the roundabout whirl violently, and he wishes Natalie would take his hand again, he has the impulse to reach for her himself, press the bones of her wrist, the length of her fingers. Instead he stuffs his hands down in the pockets of his coat and wishes for another way things might have been. He feels sorry for getting into this at all, and when they pause at a crosswalk he can feel Natalie look over at him—curious, gentle, just a little alarmed. In the dark, his face warms.

He has never forgotten all those sensors, wires, taped to Kelly's face. Taking the pulse of her brain. It was a smaller room than you'd expect, the lights off, everything sort of purple. The better to get at her forehead, someone had gathered her long hair away, piled in a twirl on the pillow, like dry seaweed strewn out on a beach.

He and Daniel and Erin stood there, shoulder to shoulder. Early hours of the morning, predawn, her parents had arrived, and somewhere they were off conferring hopefully with doctors. It would be another hour before they tried to wake her, but a nurse came to check on all the charts and screens and fluid bags, and he said it was perfectly all right to take her hand if they would like to do that.

In Owen's memory, Erin straightens up, as though it's clear she must go first. The hand sanitizer, in the corner, is automatic, it gurgles when she puts her palms out. Then she goes and links her hand in Kelly's, looking stiff and anxious, her eyes fixed down on their two hands. Daniel hesitates, then he goes to the hand sanitizer, too. The machine growls briefly, and when Daniel turns back he meets Owen's gaze, gives a small choked cough, and nearly laughs. Bleakly, Owen tries to smile, but Daniel looks away. The last time they are all four together in one place. Owen is bewildered, he takes Daniel by the elbow, knowing this is helping nothing. Erin takes a long unsteady breath, she lets go of Kelly's hand, she lets it stay there on the blanket, her own hand hovering above it. I don't know what to do, she says, in a voice that's rising, verging on panicked. She puts her hand up to her forehead, says, I think maybe we should go now, should we go now, do you think? She looks at Daniel, looks at Owen, like one of them is meant to tell her what to do. And then Owen can feel something between all of them, coming undone. Neither he nor Daniel answers, and everything is quiet, there is only this repeating beep, beep, beep, as Natalie turns in the crosswalk with an inscrutable expression. The crossing light flashes, Owen stands at the curb, his heart is racing. Are you coming? Natalie says, and she puts out her hand. The dry leaves turn over in the wind, and over and over.

You Are with Me

— — —

Here is how I came to my decision. One night Adam was making dinner, and I was making sketches in the small room that was my office. I found myself looking out the window at the snow plunging down, and thinking abstractly of warmer locales—I imagined for example a baby on a beach, scooping sand with little grasping hands.

I thought if we ever had children, Adam and I would raise them somewhere warmer. Thinking this I reached for a cup of tea he had placed for me on the desk, but when my skin touched the ceramic I was scalded. It occurred to me through my shock I was not sufficiently paying attention. I put my hand on the cold window to soothe the pain.

Around me on the desk were different floor plans I was sketching. In the kitchen, Adam was cooking a whole chicken: our apartment was fragrant with butter and thyme, lemon and roasting skin. That Adam often cooked for me was a kindness I sometimes felt I could never repay.

My pain was subsiding, but when I peeled my hand from the glass, its print stayed behind like a ghost, and on my palm a red welt rose brightly. I felt a certain clarity then— my unswayable choice. Eventually I would have to tell Adam. For now it was a private certainty I turned over in my mind like a small and unusual stone.

I thought about it all winter, working alone at my desk, while Adam went to and from the law school where he studied. All day I made renderings of buildings I would never live in, and listened to the gentle hum of our fridge in the adjacent kitchen.

At the end of each workday I would stop drawing to take a long run. One day, though it had been my intention to do a five-mile loop, I didn't turn back. I kept running, into the woods outside of town. I ran over sharp stones and through thorns. The earth was cold and hard, the bare plants and brambles sheathed with ice. I ran along the lake, where muted light glittered on its blank surface. At dusk as the light receded, I came upon a timber-frame cabin whose warm glow invited me inside. I went in, wiping cold sweat from my forehead.

Inside was a restaurant: small, cozy, empty. Sawn oak beams overhead, a pine floor, and a fireplace furnished with logs that had not been kindled. There appeared to be no waitstaff, only a grim, attractive maître d' whose eyes appraised me as I entered. The restaurant had seven tables, each furnished with a wavering candle, and for one ecstatic moment I thought I would go sit at each one. I wanted to experience which was the most comfortable— which the best distance from the kitchen—which ideally angled to take in the view over the lake. I wanted to experience everything, and then decide. Instead the maître d' gestured to a table, and I sat obediently. I ordered vegetables—braised carrots like slender fingers, the mollusk halves of brussels sprouts. I ate bread with cold butter and I drank a glass of wine, which dripped on the white tablecloth: small stains like drops of blood. When I had eaten everything, the maître d' offered me the small key to a room upstairs, which I accepted. Having climbed the stairs, I fell asleep in a soft bed that seemed to subsume me entirely.

In the night I was awoken by the sound of seven men. They were knocking on every door up and down the hall, insisting I come out and fix them dinner in the restaurant. They broke into my room and thronged around me. Soon I was downstairs in the restaurant's large industrial kitchen, brightly lit, disoriented. *Where am I?* I asked, and the maître d' kissed my hand. He said: *You are with me.* His eyes filled up with silver tears of joy. I felt I could see him imagining the children we would have together, counting up their sweet faces.

When I was again in my own apartment, I found the blankets were a nest around me, warm and creased. Adam was in our kitchen making breakfast. He never seemed to need as much sleep as I did—I needed whole hours more. If I wanted to, I could sleep till noon.

From our kitchen came the smell of bacon and buttered toast, and I felt some dim connection—as if the more Adam cooked, the more meals he set before me with his hopeful smile, the more sleep I would need. No domestic effort from me could equal one from him, I knew. He got special credit. I thought of my mother, in the kitchen of the house where I was raised: In the memory she was drinking her morning coffee, the windows still dark, her bathrobe knotted at her waist. The coffee machine hissed and gurgled. In the memory, neither of us said anything.

I got out of bed and went to our kitchen. Adam was laying strips of bacon on a plate. While we were eating what he'd made for us, I said to him abruptly: *One thing I dread about becoming a mother is never getting enough rest, walking around like this suggestion of who I used to be, wishing I was asleep.* There was bacon grease on my hands. Adam looked at me with dawning apprehension, his hand poised over a piece of toast. We had never spoken about children before, and perhaps he had made some assumptions about what I hoped for. So then I had to tell him.

That was Sunday. We talked about my choice and then, as we were both upset, Adam suggested we take time to consider our respective positions. All week he emanated seriousness and alarm when he looked at me: No children! I could see he was working hard to continue being kind, and I could see he gave himself credit for that work. One night we confronted each other in the bathroom mirror before bed. Adam said: *If I'm being honest I do want to have a family someday, and it isn't negotiable for me.* He wore an old, soft T-shirt, and a pair of blue underwear. He wore the eyeglasses he only put on before bed, and his feet were bare on the bathroom tile.

I spat my toothpaste in the sink and saw there was blood mixed with the foam. I bared my teeth in the mirror like a bear and pushed back my gums, but I couldn't locate where the blood originated. It was easier for men to idealize a family, of course. *It isn't fair*, I wanted to say, but he wouldn't understand. I only had the sense that having a baby would be one change too many, of all the changes I had made for Adam in my life.

In the mirror, our eyes met. Some impulse made me reach to turn the light off, so we were standing in shadow, silhouetted, the only sounds our breathing and, in the next room, the refrigerator humming. In the meat drawer, slipped in among the cold cuts, Adam was keeping a liver pâté in the brown paper, to eat tomorrow for our anniversary. He had bought it specially. I had watched him place it in the fridge with attentive, gentle care. And what did I owe him in return? In my mouth I could still taste the bright spearmint of toothpaste, the bitterness of blood. I said to him again, experimentally: *It's possible I don't want to have a family at all.*

He said: *You would of course have the right to make that choice for yourself. It's only fair.* I wanted him to make some request of me, but of course he wouldn't speak beyond the boundary of what each of us formally owed to the other. I could hardly make out his face in the dark as, with a sound like a small bell, he replaced his toothbrush in its cup. And then I missed him, with a keen sense of loss and absence.

I heard him go into the kitchen, I heard him throw something away. I looked into the dark mirror and I could see the possibility of a wedding in it, a small ceremony with each of our delighted families, a reception where I danced with abandon. I did not want to keep dancing but I found I could not stop: not even for a drink of water. Not even for a piece of cake. Sweat cascaded from my arms and face. As I spun, I felt sure I heard someone cry out, I thought maybe the sound was my name, I thought maybe the voice was my mother's. Her blurry figure seemed to reach for me, approaching from across the room by a tall fireplace, holding out her arms urgently. Then I was certain I could hear her voice in my ear: *Run through the woods, and don't ever come back.* But Adam was crossing the dance floor with a plated piece of wedding cake, pink-frosted sponge crowned with sugared fruit. His shirt sleeves were rolled up, his tie loose around his throat: a person who would never demand, a person who asked warmly and directly for the things he wanted most, trusting that someone would listen. His eyes were filling up with tears. He wasn't crying for joy, he told me. He dearly wanted a family, he was just very sad. And it was specifically with me that he wanted a family—wasn't that nice? Wouldn't I consider changing my mind?

He held out a bit of cake to me, on the end of his fork.

What Else Happened

— — —

I was failing Human Bio, the semester when this happened—which of course you have to pass, if you're wanting to be premed.

Up until this point, I thought I would become a doctor. My father was a cardiologist, it was spring of sophomore year, and all my life I'd been praised for being imperturbable. I thought medicine would suit me. I remember my professor saying, near the end of the semester: It's clear to me you're putting in the effort. Take a C minus, I want to help you out here.

His hands were folded on the desk, and I remember hearing, as I thanked him, how I sounded unconvincing. By then it was the end of the semester and I no longer knew how to make things sound the way I meant them. But at the time all this first started, it was still early in the semester, and I still thought: Yes. Yes I can get this grade up, yes I'll still become a doctor.

To be honest I hate describing this semester. I'd rather talk about the term before this, sophomore fall, when I had the best accent of anyone in French class. I had become less bewildered and more at ease in the subjunctive, and I could converse haltingly with my grad-student TA, which was new and uncomfortable and rewarding. My life felt simplified in office hours with her, maybe because the verb tenses I was most fluent in were simpler ones. My TA wore glasses and had a small office that looked out on some thin, clustered trees. I liked the way the lamp on her desk illuminated us, and the way she would nod with interest when I paused to formulate.

But that was the semester before this one, and now I wasn't even taking French because premed took up all my electives. I was constantly implying to people that this didn't bother me: to my father, to my French TA, to my professors. I said French was just an interest, nothing essential. I wanted them to think I didn't mind at all. I liked to appear not to have miscalculated, not to have misunderstood myself, not to have anything but the most absolute grasp on my own intentions.

It was not the best semester for me, to be honest. For one thing, there was a record-breaking blizzard—freakish for

DC—during which I fell on an icy section of sidewalk on 33rd Street near where I lived and broke my wrist. I remember slamming down hard on the bricks, trying to break the fall with my hand. I remember my backpack sliding away from me, splayed on the ice. I didn't want to be someone who would make such an avoidable mistake. When it happened, I was on my way to meet this guy I knew. We had a plan to meet up and do homework, in light of Human Bio being cancelled due to snow. He wasn't in that class, he just made time for me. When I texted him later to explain why I hadn't shown up, he seemed disappointed he hadn't been able to bring me to Urgent Care personally.

It was my left wrist that broke, which made it difficult for me to do my work in the following weeks, because of my left-handedness. Anyway, I want to tell this in the right order. What else?

To practice my French, I hoped to keep attending office hours. My former TA said she would be happy to keep meeting with me: Bien sûr, she said, *Of course*. She was natively French, she had come to DC for a masters in International Relations. I had no idea what this entailed, so I read up a little in the course catalog. It was a highly interdisciplinary degree, and I was impressed, but also afraid to ask her about it. I did spend time translating certain questions in my notebook, like *How did you become interested in this field?*, for example.

I didn't want my French to get rusty, because I had this idea I would study abroad in a French-speaking city in the fall. I devised a plan to keep going to office hours every week for practice.

Of course it didn't turn out that way, this semester being how it was. De la neige, I remember saying, meaning *some snow*, when my TA gestured compassionately at my left arm and said, Comment tu t'es blessé au poignet?

How did you hurt your wrist, or more literally, *how did you hurt yourself in the wrist?*

Employing the familiar "you," not the formal. I really liked her glasses, which were red.

This guy I knew, the one I mentioned—I sometimes got the sense he wanted to date me. Actually, looking back, it was hugely obvious, and I just didn't want to see it. The best I can diagnose myself here is I thought being able to ignore a thing was the same as its resolution, or the same as it not existing. Good thing I didn't become a doctor, right?

I guess I didn't want to lose this person's friendship. Or maybe it's truer to say, I didn't want to stop having his company. At this point I still thought anyone I got along with could be counted as a friend, which seems dumb now—really dumb.

One thing I remember is this guy, my friend, wanted to sign my cast. I told him I didn't want anybody writing on me, but then when I was reading, not paying attention, he signed his name anyway, just sort of turned in his seat and reached over. I remember feeling vaguely disturbed by this, and also self-conscious—as if someone were watching me from the corner to see how I'd respond. We were at a coffee shop, I started packing up my books. I said I was going to leave. It was hard to explain the sense of transgression, and I wondered was I being crazy. I remember I stood up, and then I sat down again. He ended up convincing me to stay so he could apologize.

Eventually we left the coffee shop and he offered to walk me home. We were standing in the light of a streetlamp at the corner of Wisconsin Avenue and I remember thinking it was a nice thing for him to offer, conciliatory, and I appreciated it. He was looking at me intently. I had the impulse to say sure, walk me home, but then for some reason didn't.

I just said, I'm okay actually, it isn't far. He looked disappointed, and I felt guilty, then uncertain why I felt that way. He said, How far? And I remember waving my hand, as if to say, Oh just over that way. I remember not under-standing why I was being vague, not understanding my own behavior even slightly.

Within a week of the blizzard, the snow started melt-ing. Around campus you started to see people on bikes again, but I couldn't ride mine, because of my wrist. It just stayed locked against a NO PARKING sign near my apart-ment. The study abroad application was due soon, so I was googling Lyon and Toulouse and Montpellier all the time, because I was thinking somewhere other than Paris for study abroad—somewhere less obvious. I liked the look of Lyon in particular: green water on the canal. But I knew I wasn't good at deciphering my own instincts, and I remem-ber really trying to understand if liking a picture meant I should actually go there.

For some reason I hadn't told my father about study abroad, even though I looked at the pictures almost daily. I was so embarrassed, back then, by the things I wanted or did not want. I wasn't sure how to express uncertainties, or possibilities. I needed people to think that whatever was happening to me, I had planned it exactly that way.

At the time I had this part-time job at a cupcake shop in Georgetown. People love cupcakes in places like Georgetown—they'll line up around the block on a Saturday, just to buy a cupcake. I was good at that job, since I was imperturbable. People would stand in line for ages, and by the time they reached the counter they'd be grouchy, but I hardly ever reacted, and I always got the orders right.

My manager said I got the job done, he'd always nod at me approvingly. The only thing wrong with me, my manager said, was how I constantly forgot to clock in. He had this tattoo on his arm that I was always trying to decode. Sometimes the guy who was my friend would come by the shop to say hi, and he'd lean against the counter and make fun of himself for being unable to choose a cupcake. Whenever my friend turned up, my manager would say to him: You again. Then my friend would joke that he was here to bother me, and my manager would laugh a little coolly.

What else happened? I did the study abroad application, I checked off first-choice Lyon, second-choice Toulouse. Something about immersion in another country felt increasingly compelling—like becoming someone else. It was probably March by then, and I still had the F in Human Bio. I failed back-to-back quizzes, it was making me crazy. Nothing I did brought the grade up, and I felt ineffectual in a way that was foreign to me. It was true I'd always had more natural aptitude for French than for science, but I'd studied hard so it wasn't obvious to people; now it was like I was reaching the limit of my ability. I remember thinking: more time and energy can fix this. I wrote up some flash cards. I drilled at it constantly. I'd take the flash cards everywhere.

I'd do them at night before going to sleep, I'd take them on walks around Georgetown, I would sit in the dining hall at meals and flip through the packet. It was slow going since I only had one hand to work with, and I needed it both for eating and for turning cards over. If I saw anyone I knew, I'd say I was too busy to talk. Now's not a good time, I remember saying to this guy, my friend, when he joined me at my table one night. I won't bother you, he promised, and sat there eating his cereal.

The cards made actually no difference. I failed another quiz, I threw up before the midterm out of sheer concern. This was something that never happened to me before: feelings to the point of illness.

Later that semester my friend would tell me something I wrote him in an email made him vomit. But anyway why am I saying this? I don't want to talk about that.

So what else? After the midterm I gave myself a break for just one night. I turned off my phone and went to a French movie at the AMC. I remember having this precarious feeling as I walked there, hugging my coat close around me. What's interesting is there was a congresswoman at the movie, I recognized her because my roommate was a congressional intern, and she had shown me a photo of this congresswoman online. The internet had a lot to say about this woman's style. She had a sculptural sort of haircut for one thing, which a lot of people loved, but other people thought it made her seem ridiculous.

I remember I stood behind her in line for popcorn and listened to her talking to her husband. It didn't seem like he was listening that closely. Then it turned out they were going to the French movie, too, and I ended up sitting behind them; I worried they would think I was trying to follow them. I was relieved when the movie started, although as it progressed it became clear I still needed the subtitles, and I had this profound sense of my own cluelessness and disorientation: I had hoped I might be past needing subtitles, I wanted to be doing better.

I remember feeling a strange intensity about this accumulating in me as the movie went on. I remember saying to myself: You have to calm down here, nothing very bad is happening.

Then on my way home, I tripped on a buckled section of brick sidewalk, which had an old tree root growing out of it. By then the snow had melted, and I honestly had no excuse. I should have seen. I landed on my stomach, flash cards fluttering around me. I broke my other wrist. So then I had two casts: one with this guy's name on it, one without. While I was getting my second cast, I should have asked the doctor if he could do something about the writing on the other one—but I didn't want to explain how I had let it happen.

As far as my right wrist, I remember that my father couldn't believe it. I called him while I waited to be seen at Urgent Care, and I think he couldn't decide if it was okay to laugh about it. After we hung up I sat there feeling mortified, imagining the doctor telling me I was pathetic, clumsy, not paying attention, not seeing what was right in front of me. The next day I ran into my friend outside the library and I remember he couldn't believe it either. He said, sympathetically: I bet you're endlessly replaying the fall. He was right about that, and I laughed, and it was sort of a relief. Then, as if to show he meant no harm, my friend held up both his hands. He said, No writing this time.

I had actually tried washing it off, when he first wrote on me—I put my whole arm in my bathroom sink at my apartment. I used up nearly a whole bottle of hand soap. You're not supposed to get your cast wet actually, and nothing I did was overly effectual, it only kind of reduced his signature to a bluish smudge—but at least you couldn't read it. I remember, when I ran out of soap, looking at myself in the mirror and wondering if I was going to cry.

One weird thing is that even in the weeks where my two casts overlapped, when I had actually no use of my arms, the cupcake shop had to keep me on. It was some sort of legal thing, maybe. I felt feverishly guilty, I kept saying I would give up my shifts, and my manager kept saying, You have to take it easy. But other times he'd say, You're getting a great deal with us aren't you?

I'd stand at the counter and try to at least say soothing and competent things to the customers, even if I couldn't do anything for them. To this day I feel guilty when I think of my co-workers because I was useless, and everyone was picking up my slack. At the end of the semester, after everything, after I quit, I ran into one of my co-workers. I remember wanting to apologize—but there's always this question of whether your apology is more of an imposition than leaving it alone, and so I didn't, I just said how are you, and we caught up without any real warmth and left it at that.

I remember her walking away across the quad afterward, running her hand through her long hair, and how I had this sense of failure. Anyway, what else.

Once I got the second cast, I knew I had to hold off on office hours for a couple weeks. I wanted to wait until the first cast was removed, at which point I was hopeful my TA wouldn't realize my one cast had switched arms. I didn't want her knowing what I'd done. I really hate describing this semester to be honest—I guess it was about six years ago now, but in some ways it feels so immediate. I wish I was talking about the next semester, in Lyon. I loved France and I was more at ease there. Living in another language made me feel far from everything, and I liked that, especially after everything that happened. I don't know why it's this semester I'm describing, when I could talk about the next one—when I was living abroad with two good wrists, speaking good French, doing well in all my classes, riding a bicycle by the canal.

The only bad thing in Lyon was how I did not want to come back to DC.

While I was waiting for my study abroad application results, I kept googling pictures of France. Certain photos I saw online reminded me of the canal in Georgetown—which, submerged below street level, felt a lot like being in another time. On warm days freshman year and sophomore fall, I used to go running along it. I had been a competitive runner in high school, and running helped me clear my head. But this semester I could only walk, because of my injuries. Strictly speaking it's not like you need your arms to run, but it's inhibiting. This guy, my friend, came with me on a few of these walks. Sometimes I invited him, and other days he'd text and ask if I was going. One day in mid-March we went walking and he finally said something about whatever was going on here between him and me. The sun behind him was bright and glaring. He took me by both my casts and explained about his feelings. I am sorry to say I thought this was nice of him. I was flattered. I hate this story.

But he said he didn't want to date me. He didn't want to change my life, he said, since he had privately arrived at the conclusion I didn't want this either. He just wanted me to know. He wanted to rest easy, he said, knowing he'd made me aware of what he felt. This was fine with me, and I somehow appreciated being told. I suppose on some level, I didn't mind the possibility of him and me existing.

At the end of this walk I remember us parting ways. I wish I could spend the whole day with you, he said, and this made me feel acutely trapped but also somehow grateful— like there was something he perceived about me that was important to who I was. He was looking at me seriously and affectionately. He said, I promise I won't bother you about this again. He said, From now on it's just cupcakes and sunshine from me.

He meant, I guess, that he intended to be upbeat and carefree. But I remember walking away from him, wondering about how I was supposed to behave now, and when I got home and looked at my phone, I already had a message from him: *Cupcakes and sunshine*, with a photo of my cupcake shop and the sun lowering down the block behind it. For some reason I wrote back: *I love it*. I felt some imperative to maintain the connection, like this was my responsibility. We had met only at the end of the previous semester, but I'll say we became sort of instantly close.

After all this happened I came to feel that instant closeness is a thing you have to guard against—a thing that can get fairly out of hand.

Another thing this semester was that I started to have problems falling asleep. I'd just lie there and think about things, which was excruciating. Eventually I started sleeping on the couch instead of my bed, so I could fall asleep with the television on, as a distraction. I had a sense this wasn't a healthy behavior, and even though I turned out to be so bad at science, I still think I'm right about that—I just imagine over time it could mess with your ability to process, or remember, or think straight.

I believed this at the time, too, only I couldn't stop doing it.

I will say I liked where I lived that year: I shared a basement-level apartment with the congressional intern, and she and I felt at home there, we became friendly. Our landlord, who lived upstairs, even let us take advantage of his washer-dryer setup, which was convenient even if a bit strange, since it involved using a spare key to go traipsing up through his townhouse, up to the second-floor bathroom. It always felt like an invasion, even though we had his permission. My roommate was sweet about helping me with laundry when my wrists were broken, and she also made me a smoothie every morning for breakfast. Then I would drink the smoothie while she took a shower and got ready to take the bus to Congress, and I'd fret about whether I was the sort of person who would do this for her, be so kind and giving, if the situation were reversed.

Questions and doubts of this nature were something I had in common with this guy, my friend, one of the things that made us close at first. It was that we didn't trust ourselves, didn't know what kind of people we were at heart, I guess, and maybe we could see that in each other. We were introduced at a holiday party for all the language departments—he studied Portuguese, and a girl I'd met in French class knew him from her dorm. We encountered him at the fruit and cheese table, and she said to me: This is John.

I know this sounds melodramatic, but I don't ever like saying his name. Once, last spring—which I guess would have been around the time of my five-year college reunion, though I didn't go—someone else named John asked me for my number at a bar, and for that reason alone I declined. This was probably a mistake. If things had worked out, or even if it had just been a nice enough evening, then maybe the name could have been redeemed. It was similar with Rory, who was on study abroad in Lyon with me and turned out to be from the same town as John. I just didn't want to have to think about that, so I mostly stopped hanging out with her.

I think John and I might have continued on as we were, without further incident, if I hadn't met Noah. As in, if it were not for the immediate test of Noah, I don't know that John's profession of feelings would have changed much.

It's not like Noah even stayed in the picture, although maybe he would have, under other circumstances—I don't know. I could speculate forever.

Noah I met through my roommate. He was also an intern in the same congressional office, and he had a car, so he'd drive her home once a week after this policy dinner their congressman did for other congresspeople at his town-house. Shannon had all these nice things to say about Noah, and then one night around mid-semester they went for a drink before he dropped her off, and Shannon texted to invite me. They were at this stodgy place in Georgetown where the Kennedys got engaged—it's famous, but I'd never been.

I think this was just before spring break, because I had gotten my first cast off and I remember holding my own drink, relieved that I wouldn't have to explain the separate origins of my two casts to Noah. Relieved, too, because when I went home for spring break, my father would not see the cast with writing on it and ask me about it. I just didn't want to have to tell the story.

I also remember I'd scraped only a D on my bio midterm, so I knew when I got home I'd have to speak to my father about this whole being a doctor thing—how it was looking so unlikely, like maybe I just didn't have the aptitude.

It turned out Noah was also a former high school runner. He asked if I wanted to go running sometime, but I said I couldn't, because having my arm in a sling made it awkward. I sort of surprised myself by suggesting that instead we take a walk. We did this. A long walk, I guess the next day, from Georgetown over the river, down to the Mall.

The memory of kissing Noah on the steps of the Lincoln Memorial is a really nice one.

I'm trying to straighten out the order of events. I went home to my father's house in Connecticut for spring break: I remember I studied a lot, and one day I had lunch with my friend Charlotte. We'd gone to all-girls school together, and I remember being kind of obnoxious at this lunch, eating my French toast, telling her how more of my friends at college were men than women. I think I saw another French movie one night when my father worked late. I texted Noah a good amount, but also John a good amount, and felt conflicted and guilty but didn't ask a single person for advice. I didn't want anyone to know about any of this until I had solved it for myself.

Towards the end of break I had this big argument with my father, who was irate that I had done the Lyon application without even mentioning it. He wanted to know why I couldn't be more open with people, why I went to such great lengths to keep things to myself. I didn't have any explanation. I said I was very sorry and he said, Okay. My father is terrible at accepting apologies. The next day I went back to DC on the train. Saying it that way makes it sound as if I stormed off, but I only mean it was the end of the break, and I had to go back to school.

While I was away, Shannon had had this bizarre experience. She'd stayed in town because of her internship, and she was pleased because our landlord, Paul, was going to be at an academic conference in Europe all week. We used to try to plan our laundry nights when we knew he'd be traveling, so we wouldn't encounter him in his living room and have to make small talk. It always felt fairly weird, just letting ourselves in like that. But when he was away it felt sort of decadent—walking freely through his house and up to the second floor, flipping on all the lights.

It turned out he'd stayed home, apparently. Shannon told me when she was turning the key in the lock, she heard him say, sort of shocked, Just a minute! Then he came and opened the door wearing only his bathrobe. She said when she passed by the TV she could see it was on, though the screen was only blue. He stood there eyeing his book-shelves while she went up with her laundry, and when she came back later that night to switch it over to the dryer, he'd disappeared.

Totally weird, I remember her saying, sort of laughing as she switched on the blender. She was making us kale smoothies, even though I had one good arm now and she didn't have to. Over the sound of ice being pulverized, she shouted, Why would you give us the keys in the first place, if you didn't want anyone coming and going?

It's not like he couldn't just tell us to go find a laundromat.

That same day, I remember I returned to office hours with Lucie. We had communicated by email about my recommen-dation letter for Lyon, and I wanted to thank her in person, and also to communicate my plan about resuming office hours, every week, without fail, starting now. I thought ver-balizing this plan might make me more accountable to it, might nudge me into having some level of integrity.

Tu t'es blessé à l'autre poignet? is the first thing she said when she saw me.

The other wrist. Even now it embarrasses me.

When our appointment was over, Lucie recommended a screening of a French film that the department was organizing—she gave me a flier and said I should come. So I texted Noah and asked him to go with me, and afterward we stayed over at his place, and in the morning we went for bagels and he walked me back home. And this is around the time when John started calling me so much, though maybe I have something out of order. I guess John's declaration by the canal must have been after Noah and I had already met—because I remember something else John said to me that day, which was: I want you to date this other guy and be happy, it seems like you really like him, and maybe you and I will have our chance some other time.

He said, For now I'm okay if you want to wait and see.

I believed him. I thought we could defer the possibility, put it aside for the moment, without corrupting present circumstances. This all seems manipulative of him now, looking back, but on the other hand I let it happen, and also, sometimes you're manipulative without knowing you're being manipulative, and in that case where if anywhere does the blame lie?

John kept asking about Noah, he sent me an email one night asking how things were going with my other guy, and I told him it was going well, hoping maybe that could be the end of us discussing it, but then he wrote back: *Your email made me so sad I was physically sick.* By this point all the trees in Georgetown were pink and flowering, their fallen petals flattened on the brick sidewalks. Noah and I were taking walks around the city together, spending nights at his apartment, and I liked how it felt waking up next to him. I had been to office hours three weeks in a row, and I was at least getting Ds instead of Fs in bio. And John would not stop calling and calling and calling me. I don't know why I always picked up, why I felt it was important to smooth this over, to maintain the connection. One night we were on the phone, and I was talking in the calm voice I used with customers if they'd waited for hours and we didn't have the cupcake they wanted.

I said, I wish this didn't have to be such a big problem.

I said, What exactly happened to "I don't want to change your life in any way?"

I remember I was in Noah's bathroom with the fan on. I was talking in a low voice, sitting on the edge of the bathtub. And John said, I guess I changed my mind. He said, Hannah, I think I'm not okay with this new guy, I think I want to win you back.

I had this instinct to turn on the water, get into the tub.

He called at least daily. Often more. I would sometimes think of the night he almost walked me home, and I'd feel this vertiginous sense of relief I never gave him my address. I decided I would quit the cupcake shop—I told everyone I wanted to be undistracted so I could pass my bio final, but to be honest I kept thinking about John showing up there, leaning against the counter, wanting to talk to me. I mentioned the whole thing to my father on the phone one afternoon, because I was feeling confused, I just blurted it out. And my father said, Listen to me: stay away from this guy.

This made me feel more violated than anything. Till then I had been trying to think about it as a pesky situation.

I went to get my second cast off, but they told me I needed to keep it even longer. Then I accidentally booked the follow-up at the same time as office hours, but I didn't even try to call and change it. I didn't tell Lucie either, I just didn't show up to see her, and then I found myself crying that night when I was trying to fall asleep on the futon, *The Daily Show* chattering at me through the blue-lit dark. On commercial breaks they were advertising a movie in which DC was under attack, all the monuments exploding and burned. In real life I could hear airplanes passing over Georgetown every few minutes, the sound began to upset me, I cried harder and harder.

This happened the next night too, at Noah's. I was inconsolable, and he kept asking what was wrong. For a while he just sat with me while I cried. But I didn't know how to explain anything as stupid as all of this.

Finally I got a letter in my campus mailbox: I was accepted to Lyon. I remember being worried they'd revoke the acceptance once the bio grade was posted, but they never did. Still, I didn't tell many people—if it turned out I couldn't go, I didn't want anyone to know what I had lost. But it felt good to get the letter. I called my father and told him the news, and this was a nice moment for us. He was happy for me and had become supportive about the idea of me going. This will be good for you, I remember he told me. He said, I'm on board. He sent a little congratulatory bouquet of flowers to my apartment the next day, and I saved one and pressed it in a book. I still have it, actually.

After the semester ended, I just went home without really saying goodbye. Only to Shannon, who bought me a bottle of sparkling wine to celebrate France. We opened it while she helped me pack up, and our full glasses seemed like the promise of leaving everything behind that wasn't easy to explain—or maybe that's just how it seems now. Going to France was an unusually solitary time in my life: I chose to be alone as much as possible. Riding my bike alone, studying alone, traveling on weekends alone. I didn't like meeting new people.

Another nice thing about Lyon was the change of phone number—I just couldn't be reached. So that was it with John. I also never said goodbye to Lucie, who by the time I came back had finished her degree and left the university. And I couldn't tell you why I stopped returning Noah's phone calls. How do I make this make sense? I just felt something by that point that I didn't want to try to name to anyone.

Shannon said not to worry. She was emptying the last of the wine into our glasses when she said, Noah will be fine. And there will be other guys. So many. All your life! There was something sinister in the sentiment: it reminded me of walking in DC at dusk, on the National Mall, the reflecting pool a long, dark tongue. And surrounded by all these solid monuments to men, as I once described them to my father—I remember I said it as neutrally as possible, but he looked at me like I was making something out of nothing. I once said something similar to Noah, and he was gently skeptical. Maybe I was being reductive: it's true there is so much atmosphere the monuments give the city, glowing like so many moons in the dark. In France, I sometimes thought of them on evenings when I biked the length of the canal back to my apartment by myself, the city lights a murky shine across the water. You had to sink so deep into a story if you wanted to make sense of it, is a thought that sometimes came to me unbidden. The idea of linguistic immersion would occur to me obscurely, and I'd seem to hear the memory of low planes above my old apartment, the encroaching whine, the promise of invasion, an inevitable explosion. I'd imagine Lyon on fire. Sunshine and cupcakes. A hand on my arm. And I'd try to think about something else instead.

I Figured We Were Doomed

—— —— ——

In the time I was dating M, I sometimes thought I must be an okay person—since his dog liked me so much and seemed to trust me, didn't seem to be receiving messages from her purer animal instincts that I was actually very bad.

Other times I knew that, of course, the dog's affection meant nothing. Naturally the dog liked me. Sometimes, at breakfast, I gave the dog pieces of cereal. On weekends, bacon.

The first time I stayed over, I sat with the dog on the bed while M was in the kitchen. I patted her ears, communicated to her with my eyes how uncertain I felt. These nerves. This near-happiness. *I know you can keep a secret*, I joked to the dog. *Thanks for being discreet.* She dropped her pink tongue from the side of her mouth, as if she found me funny.

At the time, I often experienced my okay-person-ness coming into question. Like the day my roommate received bad news from home, and I, watching her take the phone call, seeing her become upset, imagined that for a few days I would have our place to myself.

My roommate had tears in her eyes, and I pictured myself making dinner with M. Kissing him in the kitchen, then on the couch.

Plus it was always so easy for me, so instinctive, to glare at strangers on subway platforms when they stood too close, or walked too slowly: I was at home in frustration, I vented it openly. *Take it easy*, a man in a peacoat said to me once, as the F train shuddered away. *Don't worry about it*, I said, and kept walking.

I could imagine my mother saying this, too—*Don't worry about it*. Same severity, same disdain. Which was another problem with me: Why was I always prepared to blame my upbringing?

In contrast, M was endlessly kind, generous, self-effacing. It was one of the reasons I figured we were doomed.

In the swirl of a snowstorm, through the glass front of a coffee shop, I once watched him take the dog, who was not a small dog, up into his arms while I ordered for us inside. This way she would not have to stand in the side-walk salt, which irritated the soft pads of her feet. She had been wincing. He lifted her into the air, belly-up, through falling snow.

He used to say to me, *She loves you* because the dog would run to me, desperate, when I came in the door.

Or else, catching sight of me when I crossed the park to meet them, she'd bark and strain against the leash with longing. This was the summer before things ended between us: I'd kneel in the grass, and M would let her go. He'd be stuffing the leash in his pocket with one hand, and he'd reach with the other to kiss me. The dog barking with all her happiness.

Once when I was a child, I asked my mother to explain some things about dying. She imagined it was peaceful, she told me.

Honestly, I hated her for that. What is there to love in a permanent ending?

As for the future, it was difficult for me to be explicit: *I could always*, is the closest I came to saying what I meant, and I didn't even say it to M. Instead I wrote it in a note-book, and later I wrote a poem about writing it in my note-book, and then for months I wrote and rewrote my poem, so that, in time, *I could always* became this emotional shorthand—as in, *I could always do this, keep going this way, could keep being me and you.*

It was so entirely familiar to me, in my mind, I would forget he knew nothing about it. Nothing at all.

In this recurring dream I've had since then, M's dog can hug like humans do. Her limbs can bend in ways I can't explain. She barks, and then her barks turn hoarser.

One day I remember rearranging books in his apartment. Taking them from shelves, reordering them in new places. Stacking them on the floor. A hot day, late afternoon, we were laughing. When M brought me a glass of water, I kissed his face. Light warmed the room in lengthening slants.

That night, falling asleep, M rested his face close to my hair. I touched my nose into the crook of his neck. The dog spread herself, unhesitant, across us both in the dark. The strings of her ribcage were warm on my legs. The city lighting shapes over our blanketed forms.

Anyway, it didn't work out.

There's No Telling

—— —— ——

The storm was just beginning, but they kept on increasing the forecast: more snow, more snow, even more. The subway would be shutting down, schools closed tomorrow and also the next day. The wind rattled our apartment windows, as if attempting to shake some sense into them, and this added to the atmosphere of my argument with Ben. I said to him, If we can't order takeout there's no telling what I'll do. I didn't mean it: I just thought he and I needed a joke to share in, a mutual object for our irritation to light upon. A threat in the air apart from either of us. Something stupid to complain about together.

We had been planning on making pasta for dinner, and besides, the city was closing down, the streets outside our window more and more vacant. But Ben liked doing things to prove how good a person he was, so he nicely said he would get me Chinese takeout. He was like that—You don't have to be so kind, I would often say to Ben. What about humility, I would say, What about sometimes letting me be the nicest? Another problem between us at the time had to do with who to vote for in the upcoming primary. Ben intended to vote for the woman candidate, and I felt he was sort of pandering to me by always saying so.

What reaction are you looking for? I would say when he brought this up, his expression hopeful: perhaps about a future where this woman had been elected, or where I might voice admiration at his feminism. It got under my skin, how men collected bonus points for certain qualities that were simply expected of the rest of us: niceness, for example, or the ability to cast a vote for a woman. It troubled me when I could see Ben anticipate those points, his look of open expectation.

Twenty-three inches were projected, and on the latticework of our fire escape, snow was rising in fine rows. An hour ago, at the store, Ben and I had disagreed about what to stock up on in preparation for this storm bearing down upon us, that promised to confine us for days. He was an impulse shopper, and he walked along aisles adding what he wanted to our basket: ice cream, frozen pizza, wasabi-flavor chips. Later, at home, one of the bags split open, the container of ice cream rolled away across the floor, and I was a little outraged despite the fact that there had been no spill, no explosion, no breakage. It just felt like a sign that things were out of balance, and I wanted us in balance—a value that, in principle, Ben could understand. But when I said as much, he furrowed his brow like I was confusing him. He said, I think we should pick up the ice cream from under the coffee table and calm down.

I seethed. I walked out of the room and came back again, trying to burn off the feeling that was rising in me. He seemed desperate to say the right thing, and this made it worse—I felt like an animal he wanted to soothe, a horse maybe, wild-eyed, unreasonable. It was the ensuing argument that brought us to the moment when I tried to make my joke, an attempt to lighten the mood: If we can't order takeout there's no telling what I'll do—wouldn't you just die for some Chinese food? But Ben appeared to have understood me earnestly, without irony, wanting to give me something I had asked for, as if I were a ledger that could simply be balanced. Now he was in the bathroom with the door locked, perhaps to make a point, or to sit and try to understand me without the interference of my presence. We were at an impasse, not only tonight but in general. I was finding living together more difficult than I'd expected, an experience of so many traps I might fall into, so many comparisons implied between us. Often I felt like some less than exemplary piece of art sharing space with a more exquisite specimen—mostly relevant as juxtaposition, as if I'd been placed in proximity to Ben to emphasize ideal qualities in his character I myself did not possess.

Soon I heard his phone ring from the other side of the bath-room door. I leaned my forehead on the cold glass of the kitchen window and closed my eyes, because I hated being the kind of people who kept our phones with us no matter what. I thought it was important in life to be able to pass time undistracted, disconnected, separate from people's opinions flying around the internet—I just couldn't figure out how to do it. Ben had been the front man in a band before he knew me, so there were times he could lose him-self to playing the piano, or listening to an album, and I envied him that. Sometimes while he showered I could hear him singing songs I didn't recognize, songs I imagined he had written himself, songs which filled me with uneasy longing.

Now, from the sound of his voice on the phone, certain muffled jokes through the door, I could tell it was Ben's old bandmate Mara calling. She and I had met just once, at their college reunion three years ago: God I miss seeing you every day, she'd said to Ben as she embraced him, and she'd pointed out, presumably for my benefit, a table in the student center where they used to sit and eat together. To me she said, I've heard a lot about you! I knew they were often in touch, I wondered if he confided in her when we argued. There was nothing precisely wrong with any of this, so it was difficult to explain why I was so upset later that night, back in the dorm room Ben and I were sharing. I can't believe we're arguing *here*, I said at one point, sitting on the flimsy mattress, listening to extreme peals of laughter in the corridor: the sounds of people reliving the camaraderie and easy affection and simpler times of college, or so I understood from Ben, who had enjoyed his undergraduate years entirely. I said to him, I hated campus life, what am I doing here with you, I feel like I'm eighteen.

Ben had nicely given this remark his full attention. He'd said, very kindly, Do you want to tell me more about that? He had really loved college—he would never understand.

Now he emerged from the bathroom, looking happier than he'd been all day. Mara was stranded. Mara was meant to transfer planes at JFK but her flight had been cancelled. Mara had persuaded a taxi driver to take her to our place. Ben was thrilled, because Ben loved to help. He was glowing. Ben said Mara couldn't wait to see me, and I knew I should say something enthusiastic in return, that it would be the nice, right thing. Instead I told him: Okay well, I'll look for the spare sheets. Sometimes I theorized I was disturbed by Ben's niceness because it made my own less-niceness so legible, threw my qualities into sharp relief, showed how my warmth toward others was situational, intermittent, dependent on how I felt about a person, prone to cut out in certain moments like an engine dying. I said to him, Do we even have a clean towel for her? He hadn't thought of that, he said. He went off looking for one, singing to himself.

He had a spacey side that sometimes made me question if his lens on the world was reliably in focus. For example he would occasionally make reference to the detectives "Sherlock and Holmes." Listen to me, I was always saying, There is no *and*. He also had trouble remembering if our apartment was on the front side or back side of the building—he had to stop and visualize it. At times I wondered, with a sense of dread, if he noticed the important things about people, the data points required to make certain judgments of character. In my imagined museum gallery of our personalities, the two of us situated in illuminating proximity to one another, my rough attempts to remain reasonably open to people allowed for better appreciation of Ben's indiscriminate warmth to all, his good humor, his easy optimism and little skepticism. I knew I was supposed to love Mara, out of loyalty to Ben. But as I stepped on the pump for the air mattress, listening to its high whir and watching the mattress rediscover its own form, I was just thinking that I didn't want him to share our ice cream with her.

Moments ago I wished he hadn't bought it. Now it felt like something I would need to defend. I was not making much sense to myself.

When she arrived, Ben went down to meet her and carry up her suitcase. I watched them embrace as the taxi pulled away, leaving behind its parallel tracks in the snow. I heard them on the stairs, and then she was in the doorway taking off her coat. Mara looked different than I remembered. In the time since the reunion, she'd cut her hair. She wore a green sweater I wouldn't have guessed was her taste, but it suited her. She hugged me with seemingly genuine warmth. Snowflakes melted in her hair. In the past, she had never enjoyed New York, Mara told us, but she was feeling it today. Something in the air gave her an intuition she belonged. Maybe she would never leave! I gave Ben a look, but he was hanging up Mara's coat, offering her a drink. I looked down at the empty street and said, It's probably worth noting today is not a typical day in New York. Neither of them seemed to hear me.

On our windowsill, snow accumulated in a thin line, rising up higher and higher. I became aware of my own need to be alone, like a storm brewing, something that might push a notification to our phones reading *severe weather.* I said, I'm going out to take a walk before I can't—before we're snowed in for good. I did not ask if they wanted to join me, but Mara said that, honestly, she was dying to stretch her legs. She didn't have winter clothes of course, we would have to loan her some of ours. Ben gave her a pair of his wool socks, which she wore inside my rain boots. I let her wear my red hat. Ben offered to stay behind—I'll make the pasta, he said magnanimously. Mara and I traipsed off. Our feet stamped prints along the sidewalk. Her face acquired a healthy blush.

Once, when Ben and I were first dating, I burned the dinner I was making for us. It was summer, desperately hot. Ben opened my windows. Ben stood on a barstool and waved a towel in front of my smoke detector. Ben was so happy to be able to help. I sat on the floor, inexplicably on the verge of crying, and felt ridiculous. Ben said, Let me sing to you. He was still standing up there, holding the worn dishcloth. He sang silly pop songs to make me laugh. He changed the lyrics to be about us. Smoke cleared from the room. Later, sitting next me on the floor, Ben had put his arm around me. Both of us were sweating. Ben said, Honestly I think we can salvage that, and he nodded at the blackened whole chicken still seething and ruined in the open mouth of my oven. It made me laugh so much, I thought he was being funny. I put my head on his shoulder and felt calm, held, steady—the warmth of his arm through his shirt entirely comforting. But lately I'd been replaying the memory and started to wonder if he'd meant it sincerely—a possibility that came to me with more alarm than I could rationally explain. Earlier, at the store, examining a box of cereal, Ben had asked me out of nowhere what year Sherlock and Holmes was first published, and I had pointed at him with a sleeve of pasta I was holding, like I could set him straight in some permanent way. I said, Listen, we've been over this, they aren't called that. Ben said, I say it to make you laugh, Shannon! And I said, But it never does.

It was growing dark around us; Mara and I passed in and out of the pooled light of street lamps, which illuminated tall columns of whirling snow. It caught in our scarves, flew in our eyes. We kept walking. Mara wanted to tell me about the pet bird she'd had, a parakeet, back when she and Ben and all the other guys were in their band. How had we arrived at this subject? She said the parakeet was called Chirpy, that it had yellow feathers and an uncanny way of seeming to really listen to people when they spoke. She said every time she saw Ben she thought of that bird. He used to tuck it in his shirt pocket and speak to it with great care and attention, like it was a person. Ben would say to the bird: How is life treating you?

I said that sounded confining for the bird. In the pause that followed, in the city's strange situational quiet, I thought how this was exactly the sort of mistrustful thing someone like me would say. In general Ben was tired of me implying I was smarter than him, and in fact I knew nothing about birds. It was easy to think Ben could have been into Mara, back when they were in their band. Maybe I thought so because their dynamic seemed so enviably carefree—who wouldn't prefer it to all our tension and negotiation, all the things that he and I saw differently, all the times I failed to find the words to close the space between us? Of course he was too considerate of my feelings to ever be candid with me about something like attraction to someone else, so I was left to imagine it myself. From time to time I'd make a punishing exploration in my mind of some parallel universe in which whatever closeness they shared had become a relationship eventually—where it was Mara now living with Ben instead of me. You don't need to be jealous, I imagined Ben might say about this picture in my mind, this vivid and persistent intuition I felt compelled to consider as possible. Then he might say, I would never do anything to hurt you, tell me what it is that feels so awful, I want to understand.

And how could I ever explain it? Mara was searching in her pockets for something, and I felt myself soften. I was on the verge of saying sorry for being unreceptive to the bird anecdote when Mara said what she was missing: one of her mittens, my mittens. She'd put them in her pocket because she'd wanted to hold snow in her bare hands. I'm from California, this is a big deal, she'd said to me, her face rose-lit by the neon sign of a closed bodega, and I had thought this was a bit much; she and Ben had gone to college in Connecticut, after all. Now we retraced our steps all the way home—Mara apologizing repeatedly, me insisting it was definitely okay as we scanned the sidewalks. At home I unlocked the door airily, inventing reasons it was not a problem. I said the mittens were old. I said I never liked them that much. I said I needed new ones anyway! I imagined her thinking: I'm glad Ben found someone equally if not more nice than he is.

In the doorway, it took me a moment to understand what I was seeing: Ben at the kitchen table, laying out foil containers. The air fragrant with ginger, garlic, sesame, and chile. For a moment I was grateful, I loved him. Then Mara said, Oh my God, kung pao chicken! You're my hero. I felt my sentiments sour, I became defensive and irritated. I said to Ben, I told you not to, it's snowing, this wasn't necessary—everyone is trying to close up and go home, and you call in a takeout order? He was hurt, it was obvious. I saw the wounded look come over his face, and then I saw him rearrange his features like I wouldn't notice.

Oh no, said Mara, Oh no he's sad. And she started to sing a song to Ben, a song I realized was not unlike the song he once sang to me, standing on a barstool the night I burned our dinner.

I pictured the parakeet straining in Ben's pocket, long ago. I realized I hoped the bird had been peacefully dead for years, or at least had escaped through an open window, since it had no way to ask for something different than all that careful attention, attention that came freighted with sense of being a tremendous gift, *Aren't you lucky that someone is even listening.* I thought of a framed photo Ben kept on our dresser: the band at a gig ten years earlier. Ben in a T-shirt that fit him so well, with shorter hair and a younger face. Mara in a dress that showed her collarbone, her arm around him. I hated to look at it every day when I woke up, but I equally hated to ask him to move it, perhaps because I knew that he would do that, for me—prepared as he was to go on forever, checking off tasks on the list of things I asked for, never understanding. Earlier on our walk Mara had said to me, her voice alive with great affection, Your boyfriend was always such an asshole to me. He used to tell my jokes onstage at gigs, take credit for the laughs. Backstage he'd throw his arm around my shoulder and say: I was really funny, don't you think? I landed every punch line. They really ate me up.

Her cheeks were red with cold, like flowers. As she revealed this part of their history, I realized: I could not imagine Ben in all his kindness saying any such thing to me. I longed for it entirely and felt, again, ridiculous.

Steam was rising from the takeout boxes. Ben was looking at me with great interest in my feelings about the Chinese food: wanting, in his magnificent generosity, to give me all the space I needed to explain what he would not ever understand. My deferred wish to be alone came back like an alarm ringing and ringing in my ears. My eyes met Mara's, and it seemed possible she understood. I made myself a plate of Chinese food and took it to the bathroom. I thought of how Ben had enclosed himself here earlier, how reasonable he had seemed, taking space for himself, and how toweringly wrathful and impossible I appeared as I did just the same. I turned the lock and sat with my back against the tub, slipped my chopsticks from their paper sleeve, and imagined Ben banging on the door: impassioned, pleading, and annoyed. I imagined it for hours. As our bathroom window filled up with snow, it was something like I imagined it would feel to be out at sea in a boat that was taking on water. I ate kung pao chicken and listened to Ben and Mara's voices catch up. I listened to them get to know one another all over again, a long evening of mutual joy and enduring closeness—a conversation between two people whose connection was, somehow, simple enough.

Hello It's You

——— —— ———

Her professor is sorry Meg hates it here, but Meg says, *Oh, it's fine.* It is, in the sense that she's handling it: she's come to ask for a recommendation to transfer. When her letter came last April, her parents poured champagne, and Meg felt accomplished, pleased, only passingly hesitant. Now most days, after her 1 p.m. English class, she gets into bed and does not wake up until after the room is steeped in darkness.

———

When her father called last night, the ring of the phone pulled her up from a dream of vast oceany sadness, whose details slipped from her like water. She tried to make her voice sound alert as she answered. At one point in their conversation he said to her, gently, *You just have to calm your emotions and you will be fine there.* Meg stayed quiet. She did not say, *Please don't tell me how I'll be.*

———

In high school she was studious, she was responsible, she was fine, but now it's like something warm and animating is drained from her. In the fall she took long showers to avoid her roommate, cheerful Laura Heller, obviously thriving: always off to intramural tennis, a capella, play rehearsal, while Meg slept whole afternoons, sliding through blurry dreams. She filled out paperwork to move into a single room. In December her parents picked her up, and with the dean's approval she wrote final papers from the family room. *She's recuperating*, she heard her mother say to someone on the phone, as if this were a cold. *How are you*, said her father, and she pretended not to hear, raised the volume on the television.

———

It's February now, a new semester. Her professor's windows frame an expanse of vacant, snowy quad. Sometimes the weather is all Meg can say to articulate any of this: *It's so cold here*, she'll say. Last week her mother mailed her a new, warmer coat. Today Meg unsealed it from the box, laid it out across the bed.

———

Now she zips the coat up to her chin, as her professor promises a copy of her letter by email next week. *I hope you find the thing you're looking for*, he says as she is standing up to leave. Meg makes a grateful, noncommittal sound, aware she radiates embarrassment as she goes. Moments later, in the hall, trying to dig her phone out of her bag, she walks into someone getting off the elevator.

———

The girl wears a blue wool coat, she has unruly, pretty hair. *Sorry*, she says, though it wasn't precisely her fault, and they revolve around each other in a performance of improved carefulness—Meg laughing forcefully, too brightly. The other girl grasps her arm as if to navigate, then lets go. When Meg looks up she expects to see her retreating down the hall, but instead she's still there, paused, half-smiling, the clarity of her interest unsettling. The closing door slips between them; even so, Meg steps back, an impulse close to self-defense. Any time she reflects on it later (minutes, years) she won't be able to decide: Was this good instinct, a kind of intuition? Or just regular, unsubstantiated, stupid fear?

———

A much later girlfriend, the one Meg nearly marries, will say this moment sort of torments her. *Let's keep it need-to-know with exes*, Sara will say, laughing in a way that's maybe supposed to sound causal. *I don't need the details on how you and Jenny met.* And she'll say, in that same half-joking tone, *You should tell me about meeting me instead, how great that was.* Meg looks out the window behind Sara, where the light in the sky is starting to fade. *What are you looking at?* says Sara with interest, and she turns. With Sara it was a birthday party in Fort Greene, the summer Meg moved to Brooklyn from uptown. Sara in a pink dress, leaning on the bar. *Wait you two don't know each other?* says the host, putting her hand to her forehead, like this is an unfathomable oversight. And Sara says—eyebrows raised—*We don't.*

———

By the time the letter of recommendation appears in her inbox, Meg will have seen the elevator girl three times. First here in the English Department: the *"sorry,"* their physical proximity, the door like a film transition as it slid across the girl's face. The next time, forty minutes later down in the foyer, where Meg could not afterward explain precisely why she sat down and stayed there, reading, until the point when this girl reemerged: crossing the empty foyer, talking on her cell phone, not noticing Meg. Opening one of the front doors, closing it, gone.

———

(*I did see you actually*, Jenny will admit, some weeks later. She'll say, *I was being cool. I had smiled like such a weirdo upstairs, then I did it again when I saw you there, so—I just put my head down and got out. It was my sister on the phone. She said, "What's happening Jenny, you sound weird."*)

———

Everywhere on campus all week, Meg looks. It isn't the elevator girl buying coffee in the student center, not her swiping into a west-campus dorm, though Meg detours in both cases to be sure. Then over the weekend, her old roommate Laura Heller throws a party. The text reads: *Maybe you would want to come?* Meg's mother is always saying, *Maybe you'd feel better if you spent more time with people*; all evidence to the contrary, Meg retains the hope it could be true. Wearing the new coat, she is marginally warmer than she's been in weeks as she makes her way there under falling snow, crossing the total silence of the long, empty quad. Up the steps, inside, the party is dim, full of chatter, with a warm-body smell like the beach at low tide. She almost turns and leaves. Instead she pours a drink and looks around for anyone she knows, in this room with its low, sloping ceilings, its old windows thickly paned, its familiar but differently arranged decorations—this room that Laura Heller moved to after Meg moved out.

Improbably, Meg's eyes light on the elevator girl, surfacing from the shadowy far side of the room. She wears a short skirt, green sweater, and severe, lovely eye shadow (which in time, she'll dispute—*I would not ever*, Jenny will say, her laughter alarmed, incredulous, *I'd look ridiculous*, but

Meg will say, *No, you looked good, I loved it*). Meg takes a long, steadying sip, and her legs feel strange and soft. She is a new drinker this semester, has only very recently abandoned her resolve never, ever to be someone who drinks, and so the alcohol gets to her fast, and the memory of what's said here will always be blurry. (Jenny will always insist it was Meg who spoke first, who said—but this always seems so unlikely—*Hello, it's you*. Whereas Meg remembers saying a half-sentence, deciding not to finish it. Feeling herself flush and warm. Wanting to be close to and far from the elevator girl.)

———

In the year they stay together, Jenny will always be riffing on it. *Hello, it's you*, she'll say when she opens the door, or she'll pick up the phone saying, *Meg, it's you!* Meg says, *Jenny that doesn't sound anything like me*. Mostly it's a joke, a flirtation tense with affection and controversy. Something to laugh about, something to stake claims on: their origin story. Then one night it won't be funny—*I know what I heard*, Jenny will say as they're leaving her room, and Meg's enjoyment will dissolve. *You must not even know me*, she'll say in the ensuing argument—crying indulgently, sitting in the dorm stairwell. Confusingly bereft, head in her hands, rain pounding on the skylight several stories up. Jenny will sit beside her and move her hand in gentle circles on Meg's back. *What the fuck*, she'll say, *Of course I do*.

———

But Meg remembers this part clearly: Jenny explaining she's in a play with Laura Heller. Meg says, *How is the play?* and Jenny says, *Oh God, so bad, but it's too late to quit. They'd be stuck if I left now. Believe me, I've considered it.* They take a pair of shots. They sit together on the sill of Laura Heller's window, which has a cold draft sifting under it. Meg can recall condemning, not discreetly, Laura's taste in general—*I hated that poster, when we were roommates,* she says over the music, into this girl's ear, pointing.

———

They kiss—Jenny, who hasn't even yet told Meg her name, making the move to push one hand up the side of Meg's neck and jaw and into her hair. Meg leans back against the window so the girl can move in closer, and the cold glass through her shirt is excruciating on her shoulder blades, the knots of her spine.

———

Her hands in this girl's hair. The girl's hand moving down Meg's forearm, then her waist and her leg, as they kiss for the length of a song, then another, then part of a third until the girl pulls back, and says—trying not to smile, maybe, her shirt sort of askew and so close Meg admires the dark eye shadow—*Want to go to my room? I live upstairs.*

———

She holds out her hand, a joke, as if to shake hello. *I'm Jenny.* Then she raises her eyebrows: So? And actually Meg does want to go—but also she wants to stay where they are. Significance floods her, and briefly she imagines the cold from outside enveloping the room, their breath in clouds, ice forming in Jenny's hair, a preservation. Lately any time Meg calls home and tries to explain, her father tells her, *Life is change.* Her mother says, *You'll be all right.* Now Meg is shivering, agitated by this sense she has had so often lately that something essential is leaching out of her. *Come here*, she wants to tell this girl. *Stay here.* Instead she nods more or less normally: Yes. And she takes the girl's hand for the joke, small and warm.

———

While the elevator girl—Jenny—hunts for her purse on the shadowy far side of the room, Meg hovers by the door, shifts her weight from one foot to the other. Jenny is telling a handful of friends she's leaving. She pushes her unruly hair behind her ear, looks pointedly over her shoulder. So now all the friends' eyes move to Meg, by the door. She tries to shift her own gaze casually to her phone. Tries not to signal Laura Heller is the only person she knows here, opts to suppress the question of whether she is doing something stupid. A text from her father resolves on the screen: *Good night.*

Out in the hall then. Their paired, padding footsteps on the dimly lit concrete stairs. *Sorry for my dumb friends back there,* Jenny is saying. They kiss more on the landing, Jenny's hand just touching Meg at the side of her face, the cinder block wall on Meg's back, then Jenny's, and now Jenny is fixing her hair again, unlocking her door, making a small performance of this, like they're in some old movie: *Won't you come in?*

The door swings open, it's dark inside. Jenny shakes her hand free from the sleeve of her coat, reaches her fingers to flip the light switch. (But actually that's Meg's coat she's wearing, which seems premature, and what's more they never went outside on this night, only upstairs from second floor to fifth. So this part is misordered, transplanted? This part is another time. On another night entirely, Jenny is saying, in that same old-Hollywood voice, *Get in here, would you?* Taking Meg by the wrist, drawing her closer.)

But this part Meg remembers, this is clear: a tentative snow in the half-lit dark outside the window. She remembers lifting Jenny's shirt over her head, Jenny saying something and laughing. Jenny's snaky ribs, this nervous closeness. Later, the streetlight seeping in through fogged glass over Jenny's small form. Her tangled long hair, taking over the pillow like a weed.

———

Meg likes, as they fade into sleeping, the intimacy of all this hair—so close to her face it's practically up her nose. Likes the square of light on Jenny's cheekbone from outside, and her sleep-muttering, the sharp certain tossing of her head thrown back on the pillow. The seethe and clank of the dorm radiator, and the footsteps and low voices, brief laughing and shushing of roommates in the common area. The line of gold light under the door, and then how it goes away.

———

In the dark, both of them breathing. All night as they turn in their sleep, knocking around together like two small boats. This bed will never be enough room for them, it will always be uncomfortable, but Meg loves it entirely, possessed by a nostalgia that infects her straightaway. Cold through the drafty window. Pink-patterned sheets. One pillow shared between them, until they go and buy a second one some weeks later—which, even this early, Meg will feel is sort of poisoning the way things had once been. Jenny tossing and turning: this thing she has about which sides of herself she can and cannot sleep on, and why, why not. Meg's thing about hating to sleep by the wall, her insistence on the possibility of extrication. She has a memory of Jenny in her worn-out high school track shirt, sometime later this semester, out of bed with a towel on her arm saying, *We could literally move my bed, if you hate your side so much.* Meg says into the new pillow, *But I don't want to move your bed.*

———

In New York, five years later, Sara's bed will be objectively better. Warmer, more spacious, of course. Meg will sometimes joke, *Remember college? Remember twin beds?* And Sara will laugh and say, *I really try to forget.* The first summer they're together, in Brooklyn, the year that both of them are twenty-five, they forge a kind of ritual from the awful heat of Sara's room: drinking cold wine with a whirring box fan pointed toward them, stretched out on this bed with its nest of too many pillows. *No, don't throw them away*, Meg will say, when Sara tries to prune a few, *I like them all*, and Sara will laugh and say, *You never want anything to go.* Most nights Sara's dog will sleep between them. They wake up in the night and laugh and feel irritated and push the dog's sleeping weight around the bed. On several bleary mornings, they make a joke of gently shaking their fists at the dog together: *Stop being difficult, you jerk. Stay still, stay.*

———

Here is where they take each others' clothes off. Here is where they lie checking email on their phones, feet touching.

Here is where they go to sleep seething, any time they fight. Here is where they face each other one late-summer night, Sara's roommates' video games blaring sounds of carnage and loss and *game over* just past the closed bedroom door, a warm wind moving swiftly in the window. The dog resettles his chin on Meg's bare ankle, as Sara fixes a loose piece of Meg's hair with her fingers and says, half-kidding: *You and I would have three kids, obviously. Two would be predictable and honestly dull.* Meg laughs and moves her hand along Sara's wrist. She feels, exquisitely, hope.

———

This same summer when she first meets Sara, Meg looks up Jenny Evert on the internet—a habit she thought she'd broken but that seems, again, to beckon, to wrap its hand around her wrist. *Come here.* Jenny Evert has moved to Austin, Texas, she does marketing for a community arts nonprofit. It could be that she's dating the woman in this photo, whose arm is around Jenny's waist. To look at this picture makes Meg feel vaguely ill, time overtaking her in a nauseous wave. Then she imagines what if Sara walked in now, and the itchiness of guilt overtakes her. *Please stop talking about all these stupid things*, she remembers Jenny telling her on the phone once—just after Meg transferred to Columbia, when they were taking the bus back and forth on weekends. *I worry about you, like you'll never enjoy your actual life. You never let anything go.* Even now Meg can still replay each word, subtly accusatory, quietly furious, like the memory of a curse being placed: *You never stop dwelling on all your old stuff.*

———

And this is going to sound bad, but whatever—I don't want to not enjoy my life, because of the way that you are. I don't want you dragging me down.

———

From the beginning, they fight—it's embarrassing, shocking. They argue in public, or else alone in one of their rooms: draining, circular conversations, discordant and cruel, slipping beyond their control. *Don't be so stupid*, Jenny will tell her sometimes, pacing like a provoked animal. All her life Meg will be ashamed to remember the mutual, ready animosity—beginning so early, even the first morning after the first night, both of them sleepy, warm, Jenny reaching her hand to untwist the sheet where it's caught around Meg's shoulder, and saying with a kind of hesitation in her voice, *I've sort of been imagining running into you all week*. And then something unclasps, and Meg finds she can't contain this panic, billowing. *I don't want you to imagine me, she says, I'm a real person, I have a whole life. You only just met me.* Jenny takes her hand back. Her hair is messy around her face, she looks injured. *Of course*, she says, *I know*—but Meg is seized by a fretful compulsion to say well this was nice but she's going to leave. She starts to sit up but can't quite free herself from the sheets. Jenny says, *Hey, I was being romantic.* Meg says, wresting her own foot from a tangle of blankets: *Look maybe you won't understand this, but I don't want you to act some special way. Let's not be people who pretend.*

———

I'm going to go shower, says Jenny. *I don't really know what we're talking about.*

———

Sun through the window over the place where Jenny slept. Meg reaches for her coat draped over the desk chair, for her phone in the pocket (*warning, low battery*), where she finds in her inbox an email from her professor with, see attached, her letter. She waits for the sound of the tap coming on in the bathroom before she opens the attachment, in which she is praised especially for her passionate responses to assigned readings. This is a commendation so mysteriously saddening that she turns off her phone without reading anything more. By the time Jenny comes back, Meg has both her hands over her face. *Hey,* says Jenny then, softening—wrapped in a towel, her hair wet. She sits down on the edge of the bed, puts her arm around Meg's shoulder.

———

That night Meg is in the library, methodically entering full name, date of birth, address, into application forms, when

Jenny texts. *Come over? Or I'll come to you?* Meg logs out. She calls home while she walks, because she was supposed to call this weekend. Tonight the calm certainty in her father's voice bothers her strangely, as she picks her way over the snowbanks of the hushed campus moonscape. *Anyway I should get back to these applications*, she says, and waves her ID to test if it can swipe her into Jenny's building.

———

Help, no card access! You have to come get me.

Hello it's you! I'm coming.

———

Good night, says her dad. *Take care.* Waiting for Jenny to open the door, Meg thinks of what her mother said, all but sternly, just a few weeks earlier: *If you're this unhappy, I think something has to change.* The two of them in her mother's closet, familiar-smelling, with its wool sweaters, its folded pants, its green ceramic dish of loose change and jewelry. Looking for extra, warmer socks Meg can take back with her, because of the cold. Her mother reaches a hand to search around a high-up shelf: *There's no reason to stay anywhere that feels this bad to you*, she's saying. Meg looks down at her own feet on the floor of her mother's closet and feels a familiar sensation of illogical hope that sometimes flutters up through all her dread—a passing belief in the potential for some shift or transformation. She runs her finger along the lip of the ceramic bowl. She says: *When do you know for sure it's too late for things to get better? When do you know that you just have to move on?*

———

The night she and Jenny have their most brutal fight, she'll remember that question. They argue for hours in Meg's apartment near Columbia—her roommate at the library, the two of them liberated to storm around, to call each other names. Eventually they're tired, finally stalled, Jenny silent on the edge of the bed, Meg on the floor looking up at the ceiling. *How can you know if something is fundamentally bad*, Meg says finally, *Versus only currently? How do you know if something is temporary, or if it's the way it will always be?* Jenny will deflate back into the heap of Meg's unmade bed. She'll seem to think about that, to linger on the brink of some response, but she will not, in the end, say anything, and the two of them will lie in silence as the evening deepens into blue, and the traffic in the street keeps up its clamor.

———

Through all the hours of this argument, Meg has pulled and pulled and pulled at a loose thread in her sleeve, so much it gets unraveled around her wrist. Eventually Jenny gets up from the bed and say she's going to take a walk, she wants to be alone. She's leaving as Meg realizes in a wave of pure, giddy, furious irritation: she'll certainly have to throw this sweater away. It would be gratifying to burn the sweater on the fire escape. To shred it with scissors. To consign it fatally to the kitchen trash. Instead, alone with the muted clicking of her radiator, she sits up and lifts the sweater over her head. Carefully, she folds it into a plastic bag, so she won't forget to take it somewhere to be donated or recycled or whatever. But then it's like fuck it, and she takes the scissors and does cut up the whole, soft shape—surgically, over the trash, an experiment in destructiveness that leaves her crying so much her face aches, crying so much she imagines what if Jenny could hear her from the street. Afterward, she falls asleep on her bed, its mass of sheets. Jenny comes back later, asks her, Do you want a shirt? But Meg pretends that she's still sleeping. Jenny lies down, turns off the light, and puts her hand on Meg's back.

———

It's when Meg is following Jenny to her dorm room the second time ever, in the weird glowy light of the dorm stairwell, that it occurs to her to say something about transferring. Not yet though, she decides—pleasurably woozy, back in this girl's company. Smoothing her fingers along the blue metal banister, feeling her face warm in the new heat of indoors. It would be premature.

———

But then they spend the next—what was it, five nights together? Three at Jenny's, one at hers, Jenny's again. *We could make a bad habit of this*, Meg is saying, unwinding her scarf, as Jenny lets her in the second or third time. *Or else the best habit ever*, Jenny is saying, and kissing her, as Meg is slipping her hands, still trailing the scarf, around the back of Jenny's neck.

———

The sixth night she lies she has an assignment: *I really shouldn't. I have to write this paper.* At her desk as she drafts the personal essay for her applications, she can see the snow that crowns the hill outside her window turn gold, then lavender, then bleak gray, until the rural darkness blots it out—all but one eerie swathe of glow from the nearest campus blue-light box. *I am looking for opportunities to feel better.* Backspace, *be warmer.* Backspace, be serious, *pursue my education in an urban setting.* She closes her phone in her desk while she works. It rings once, a muted trill: her father, the voicemail says when she listens eventually. Just saying hi and he'll try again tomorrow. And here is a text from Jenny, waiting: *I want to play this cooler than I am, but I wish you were here.*

———

Somewhere, in the sinuous walkways of the dark campus, happy laughter rings. The text scares her, she doesn't know why. Curled on her side on the bed, she deletes it.

The next day, in the dining hall, she doesn't answer her mother's call. Not the day after that, either, walking back from French, though the phone rings literally in her hand as she's texting *Tonight?*—her gloves precarious where she's wedged them between her arm and ribs so she can type. To her mother, she writes: *Can't talk but I'm fine, I'll call soon.* In the morning her father calls, but she's in Jenny's kitchen and doesn't answer that, either: Jenny barefoot in running shorts, her faded sweatshirt slipping from one shoulder, cold light illumining her jaw and hair as she measures out coffee grounds with a spoon. *I can't wait for this coffee*, she's saying. A roommate emerges, wincing, and greets Jenny in a low voice, before she notices Meg and adds with an effortful summoning of interest, *Hi.* Meg starts to respond, but with a movement of her hand the roommate insinuates she's too hungover to converse. She carries herself to the shower, snaps the bathroom door shut behind her. Jenny brandishes the spoon after Dana—or was it Ellen? Well, one of them. In a low voice, she says, *Rude. Next year: a single room. Think of it. We'll be alone.*

She says it again: *Alone.* Does this suggestive, amazing thing with her eyebrows that makes Meg burst out laughing, and decide not mention she has no plans to be here next year.

———

Jenny will always be making this sort of remark: *Next year* and *after we graduate* and *someday*. One night, walking together to Meg's room, Jenny behind her as they move along an icy bit of narrow sidewalk, snow encroaching from each side, Jenny says, *Sometime we should live together, and then it won't always be like, do I even have clothes I can wear tomorrow?* Meg laughs softly: *You can wear my clothes.* Jenny says, *That would be sort of cute. Okay, I like that idea.*

———

Sara says, *Hang on*, and looks up from the fridge. She says, *Seriously?* Because it makes no sense, Meg and Jenny, barely knowing each other a month and talking like that. Meg says, setting the last dish to dry in the rack, wringing out a sponge to wipe down Sara's counter: *I know—sometimes I feel like I must be remembering things out of order. But I think we were just super young? Things move fast and you're an idiot.*

———

Sara says, *No I mean like are you actually telling me this? I mean what was this—six years ago?* Meg says, *Oh*—and it feels like there's some explanation to make, but her mouth can't find it. *Let me do that*, says Sara, and it's vicious somehow, the way she takes the sponge. The drag of her short fingernails over Meg's wet palms.

———

In the play, Jenny is wonderful. On a folding chair in the dark black-box theater, Meg is thrilled, small shivers course her spine, she wraps her arms around herself. She feels gripped with possibility, she regrets having come here with Dana and Ellen and Ellen's boyfriend—the three of them in chairs to her left, their intermittent and distracting whispers. She wishes she'd come tomorrow, had come alone. She misses an essential plot point of one scene, just imagining this other way it could have been. She twists her hands together in her lap. Distracted, afterward, she forgets her gloves under her chair.

———

And she hates having to greet Jenny in the company of others, having to share her. She can't speak: Jenny, striking in her stage makeup, is buoyant, is joyful, is embracing her friends, some of whom Meg recognizes. She's wearing the green cardigan, hair gathered up at the back of her neck, and someone's given her a bunch of daisies in green tissue and clear plastic, which she has in her arms as if holding a baby. Laura Heller materializes. Meg tries to summon something of her performance—*You were so good*, she tries, and Laura's thanks are effusive. She points at Jenny's lipstick on Meg's cheek: *You guys are cute.*

———

Years from now, Meg will run into Laura Heller at a party in Brooklyn. They will be happy to see one another, will entirely enjoy catching up. Eventually Laura will say, as she opens another beer for each of them, *I always felt responsible for you and Jenny Evert meeting*, and she will look faintly proud of herself, and Meg will be surprised by the savageness of her own reply, and the way it makes Laura's face go blank, humiliated: *You absolutely weren't.*

———

After the play there is a basically torturous group dinner that Laura has organized, at the BYOB sushi place off-campus. *We don't have to go*, says Jenny, putting on her coat, though plainly she intends to. At the restaurant everyone seems to be friends with everyone: roommates, castmates, roommates of castmastes, everyone Jenny knows, it feels like, talking over one other, passing huge cheap bottles of wine down the table.

———

So it isn't until afterward that Meg gets Jenny alone long enough to say anything. And this was the "I love you": on College Avenue, outside the sushi place. Cars easing by, their lights catching the shimmer of heaped curbside snowbanks. Still in the crook of Jenny's arm, these daises in paper and cellophane, the plastic crinkled between Jenny and Meg's two coats. Meg's bare hands in Jenny's hair, and Jenny, joking: *So not, ultimately, such a terrible night for you?*

———

Later, Jenny's falling-asleep breath is even along Meg's collarbone; she seems asleep, but then *I love you* she says again, and moves her hair out of her face, settles herself closer, touches her forehead to Meg's shoulder. Meg stares fixedly into the shadowed form of the daisies bunched together in their cup—visible over Jenny's head, as if an outgrowth of the hair.

———

A slant of streetlight through the window falls over Jenny's nose and the daisies in their drinking glass and makes, through the water, a murky amoeba of faint light on the surface of the desk. Meg has an impulse to ask who the flowers are from, but doesn't. Long after Jenny really does fall asleep, Meg wonders in the dark, considers in turn every person she saw tonight. Certain possibilities upset her. *Jenny?* she says finally, but Jenny doesn't stir.

———

Meg moves her face away from Jenny's hair so she can breathe. Wants a glass of water but can't get up, because she's next to the stupid wall. *The thing is*, Jenny says to her in the dining hall the next morning, or maybe the one after—some morning that week, anyway, plunging her fork into the soft yolk of her poached egg—*I don't know why you have to ask me that way. So suspicious. Like*

I could ask you why you didn't bring me flowers. But I didn't, you know?

———

Then someone they know passes by their table, and Jenny brightens to hide what's going on. Waves.

———

Meg goes home for a weekend. Her father is making pasta, her mother setting the table, when Meg asks, *When are you supposed to ignore what you're afraid of, and when are you supposed to pay attention?* In general, she's been wondering, is it better to ask a question if you're afraid you know the answer—is it better to get what you fear out in the open? Or should you leave it alone and hope the thought will go away—hope it won't persist, becoming increasingly complex, obsessive, tangled, confused? *What exactly is it that's concerning you?* her dad asks, and he starts adding capers to the sauce, angling the small glass jar. Meg's sitting on the counter and wants to explain her state of mind, but can't exactly. She kicks her heels against the loose door of the lower cabinet. *Careful,* says her mother.

———

At some point she realizes she shouldn't wait any longer to tell them. Outside the library, pacing the gridded, neat courtyard, tucking her face down into her scarf, she calls home. It's snowing again, of course—the afternoon daylight flat and strange through low clouds. *How nice,* says her mother. *You sound better. Will we meet her when we pick you up at spring break? Why don't we all have lunch?* Below, down the hill to the quad, Meg can see the knitting and unknitting lines of other students: crawling to class, from class, library, dining hall, gym. After she hangs up, on her way to Jenny's room, taking the stairs down the long hill—cradling her bag close, because this wet snow is coming down hard now—she already misses the time before she told them. When Jenny was only hers. She shakes her head as if to disperse the feeling, but it seems only to squeeze her more tightly. And here is Jenny walking toward her: head bent. Her hair starred with caught bits of snow. They're inside before Jenny notices anything: *Oh,* she says finally, *What is it, what's wrong?* Meg says, *I don't know, I don't know.* She frees one of her hands from its glove and holds on to Jenny's arm, wanting to tether them to each other, to this moment in time. Slush from their boots is already resolving to pooled water around them, the snow in Jenny's hair changed to shiny dabs of water.

———

Upstairs, in Jenny's room, they hang their coats, scarves, gloves to dry on the desk chair, on the radiator, by spare hangers from dresser drawers. They put their boots together to dry on a towel. In the bed, they lie close: Jenny on her back, hair damp, reading this play she has to finish for tomorrow. She has the book in one hand and the other arm around Meg, who has her French workbook open on the quilt to her assigned conjugations. She takes her pen and draws little swirls and jags, pulses in the margin. The radiator clucks, then sighs. Meg says, finally, *Do your parents know about me?* She can feel Jenny shift then, her breath on Meg's hair and the back of her neck. *Um yes*, says Jenny, sounding happy. Later that night, in the common room kitchen, Meg will tell her about transferring. Jenny will clench a hand around her glass so hard the water she's drinking will shiver in its cup, and Meg will stand instinctively. *Stop*, she'll say, *Just wait*, but Jenny is already talking, voice ragged, rising, insistent, changed, like someone else, like not Jenny at all, she says, *So many people want to go to school here. Do you know that people want to go to school here? Honestly. What is actually wrong with you?*

———

Sara will ask Meg to meet her parents when they have only been dating a few weeks. The two of them drinking Bloody Marys on an overcast Sunday at some brunch place in Crown Heights. Meg will say something about remembering to call her parents, and Sara will swirl her ice with her celery and say, hey speaking of parents, why doesn't Meg come out to New Jersey next weekend?

———

Jesus, Meg will say, unexpectedly saddened. As if something is ending too soon. Later, she'll be unable to decide if Sara's behavior in this instance shows her to have solid instincts or betrays a fundamental recklessness. *What if we hadn't worked out*, Meg will ask through a mouthful of toothpaste, however many months later. Brushing her teeth, wearing one of Sara's sweaters, coming to stand in the doorway to her room. *We might still not work out*, says Sara, sitting on the bed, stroking the dog's forehead so its eyes wink closed. *I just thought it might make you happy to be asked.* Behind her in the window the afternoon light is bright and clear, and Meg knows what Sara wants to hear: *Of course we'll work out.* Actually, Meg wants to hear it, too. But before either of them can say anything, Sara's roommate comes home. *Hey hey*, he says pleasantly, as he hangs up his bike helmet by the door. And it seems easier to say nothing.

———

When Ellen comes home, Meg is disappointed. She and Jenny have been curled around each other on the couch. Earlier they started a movie but, *You're missing the whole thing* said Jenny, once she noticed Meg looking out the window at the snow as it fell. Half amused, Jenny has paused the television, and now they're just talking, watching the snow. And Ellen is interrupting in the doorway, stomping ice from her boots, stripping away wet layers, going on about how oh, she loves this movie—what were they watching, even? Usually Meg can summon up old details, but in this case she doesn't have it. Nothing but an onscreen image, paused: some landscape, rugged. Impossible to place.

———

We have homework Jenny lies to Ellen, before they retreat to Jenny's room, close the door, fall on the bed laughing and shushing each other—which is why, in joking despair, Jenny says *But homework!* as Meg is reaching for her. *Maybe for you*, says Meg, kissing Jenny's face, her neck, moving the edge of her shirt to reach her collarbone: *I'm on my way out. No consequences.*

———

She means it as a joke, but Jenny presses her forehead to Meg's shoulder and stays there, very still. Months later, she'll look at the acceptance letters lined up on Meg's desk with feral anger—like she could kill them with her teeth, the perfect envelopes.

———

They try staying together. Her parents say, *For a place you really hated, you're still spending so much time there.* When she and Jenny break up, Meg figures it will be a sort of trial thing. An experiment of some protracted agony, involving regular check-in phone calls. Later an agreement to stop texting, to give each other space. Then Jenny taking the bus down to Columbia, where they will find that time apart has eased their problems. Just imagining it floods Meg with warmth. But this, actually, will be the last time they ever see one another: Jenny, not crying, hails a taxi on

Amsterdam Avenue. Her right hand raised in the air, one early morning.

———

Sara's parents live near the beach. On the bright fall day Meg goes to meet them, the dog comes, too. Meg walks with Sara and her parents by the water and they let the dog off-leash, watch it run the scalloping shoreline, muscles roiling. Sara's mother takes Meg by the arm so they can walk together. She says, *We're so happy to be meeting you.* After the beach Meg and Sara will sit in the sun, on the cold brick terrace next to the house. They'll clean sand from the dog's feet while it stands, sun-warm, alert to something down the beach. They'll stay together with the towel rumpled on their laps and let the dog run to the fence, where it glowers at a distant point in the trees, some far-off movement. The wind whips up around them, and Meg takes Sara's hand to move her closer. Her hand is small and warm, they lean their heads together. The cold wind makes Meg shiver, and she imagines if they stayed this way, very still in low dusk light, like something dipped in amber. She wants to say, *Stay here.* The dog comes over then, it nudges its head on Sara's lap, it gives a longing grumble. *I'm extremely cold*, says Meg at last, and Sara laughs her beautiful, porous laugh. She wraps her arm around Meg's shoulder. *Be warm*, she says, *Okay? Be warm.* The dog lets out a short, demanding sound, as, memorably, Sara tips her face up to the sun.

We Can't Explain

— — —

We're in a café together when this sudden, thunderous downpour starts up. Rain moves in long sheets down enormous glass windows. It's surprising and beautiful, nothing ominous about it. And I don't want to leave you, though I'm worried I'll be late for my family, as you and I laugh at these texts from my older sister—don't exactly remember why laughing, something about, *Is she stealing this cab? Are the police coming after her, are they tailing her downtown from the Upper West Side?*

If memory serves, I leave you and take a cab alone. I'll meet you in Brooklyn after dinner, I tell you—parents on West 12th Street, easy to get the Q to yours from Union Square.

Can't remember us kissing goodbye in the rain, so next thing I'm upstairs at my parents', having of course a drink— remember this later when it comes to the part with *Were*

you drinking, we can smell it. Dad's sixtieth, but I'm drawing a blank on his gift, except—oh, it's this photograph.
My mother's idea. My father loves our stretch of West 12th,
and so we give him, for his birthday, my mother, my older
sister, me, on West 12th, in a frame, the brickwork rising
up behind us. You and I spend the night before the photo
shoot at my place in Bushwick, take the L in the morning,
kiss goodbye in the station, before I go west to the Village
with my pink canvas bag of possible photo outfits and you
catch the Q. In the photo, as it's turned out, I am a little
too casually dressed: jeans and this plain linen shirt. Long
hair unkempt. A better daughter would be better prepared
and would not show up late. Regarding the ultimate photo,
now wrapped for this dinner, my sister has been all day
texting, incredulous that of our many options Mom picked
this one to blow up and frame? Sister feels she looks stupid
here, and true there are photos we like better, but with various objections, too—for example, *Doesn't that one seem
like it's all about me?* says our mother, who eventually goes
ahead and orders a different photo, the photo she feels like
ordering, the photo my sister hates.

So now we're all here and drinking champagne. Both
daughters have made it to the Village in this downpour.
Our mother wants to know, *Should we do cake and the
present before dinner, not after?* Dinner's in Brooklyn
and afterward, she guesses, I won't want to come back to
Manhattan, only to return to Brooklyn again to get home?

But dinner's in a different part of Brooklyn from mine, and I say no, I don't mind, which is true since the Q train's nearby, and this is my plan, though of course I'm not about to say so.

(And writing this now, I'm finding I actually can remember you and me kissing goodbye. This memory resolves, and in it, we're not outside the café. I'm not hailing any cab in the rain. In the version of this story that is true, there is no taxi I ever took alone. Instead, the downpour lets up, and we walk the rain-washed evening streets from East Side to West together, and say goodbye, see you later, at the front door to my parents' building.)

After champagne, a cab to Peter Luger Steak House, where the sixtieth birthday dinner proceeds unremarkably. My father for years has been telling one story about this place, in which it's the eighties and he's ordering steak. In the story the waiter keeps saying, *Sir are you certain you want the most spicy*, and our father keeps saying he's sure, and the waiter keeps checking, and my father keeps confirming, and then steak arrives and in fact it is entirely too spicy, this being the point of the story, and maybe the only case ever for my father of anything being over the top, too much to take. I can't remember what we're saying tonight while we eat our birthday steaks, though I do remember how it's too cold in the air-conditioning, and how dinner has this (not atypical for us) sharpened edge. Then later,

More wine? and I put my hand on my glass—where to assign blame for the part where I am persuaded to take it away?

Next thing I have here for sure, we're in a cab on our way back to Manhattan when on purpose some guy runs his bicycle into the car. Trying to start a whole thing with the driver. It's scary, and we can't explain it. The bicycle guy is shouting, he follows us for blocks, rams his bicycle a second time into our cab. So now the cab driver is angry, distraught, is ready to chase this guy down with the car, with us in it, but my parents say, *He's crazy, we're on your side. Just stay calm!*

He's crazy, he's crazy. They keep saying, *He's crazy, we're on your side.* And my chest is tight and the cab driver still muttering, angry, but he makes a right off 6th Ave, drops us off, we get out of the cab, but this isn't the part of the night that upsets me. At the apartment, cake and this present. Framed photograph, large and mediocre, unwrapped. My father could be thanking my mother more warmly, more attentively, more. Whereas you and I are different, are kind to one another, except for the times we both get confused because I get distraught can't calm down freaking out. I am like my mother, explosive: able or likely to shatter violently or burst apart. Blow up that photo. Remember, one time not long before this, me shouting on the sidewalk after storming from a bar? A passerby making a joke, and

I yell after her *Fuck off,* and you ask, without judgment, why I think I just did that?

Cake's finished now, and here's me saying tentatively that I'm going to head out. Presumably they think to my apartment and I don't disabuse them, don't tell them actually the Q, actually your place, though I feel a little guilty leaving them, even though the birthday's winding down, even though it is, so to speak, my life. Even though you love me, even though everyone here is getting fairly surly. It still feels like I'm betraying them.

And this last I remember is the crux of it, my mother wanting to know do I want to take a cab? *It would be faster.* I tell her it's just about the same, and thanks. She says, *Then which should you take.* She says, *We will pay for whatever.* I say I'm not sure but I'll figure it out, I've got this, but still she needs to know which will it be. I'm putting on my coat saying, *Why are we discussing this, I'll decide on my own once I leave.* It's just that I have this plan to take the Q, I don't say. It's just that I have certain hopes of my own. She's asking again, angrier. Years of this, okay? The same. Which will it be? Why won't I tell her? *We will pay, we will pay,* but I lose it, I say, *You have no idea where I'm going,* and how to explain the years of this that get me kicking and kicking the apartment door into the hall. (This birthday was months ago but you could, if you knew where to look, still locate the scuff marks I lashed all across the inside of the door. Then more of them out in the hall, like long smears of ink—the way they're struck into white plaster, at the top of the long flight of stairs in descent.)

You did the right thing and are a good neighbor, my sister will say later to the fourth-floor neighbor who calls the police, who reports what he thinks must be an assault, based on the sounds he hears from upstairs.

Only a family disagreement, I tell them downstairs, outside, because I'm downstairs, outside now, have been circling the block.

Were you drinking, we can smell it, they say to me—before they go upstairs to this apartment, to my family. My sister will say later, *You should have seen Mom's face. She's opening the door, and she's got this scotch going, and here are the cops.*

There is nothing to report. There is only a family. No one is hurt. I am allowed to go home: the police say I can leave, and then the police leave themselves. My sister tells the fourth-floor neighbor, *The person who's been making all that noise does not live here and is gone now.* I get on the phone in Union Square. I tell you I'm not taking the Q, I should not come over, I do not want you to see me this way, I've had this terrible time with my family. You express how you'd like to be able to be there for me. Years of this, and how will I explain to you? It's early summer, and we're in love. It's scary and we can't explain it.

I don't remember if I take the L train or a cab. After this my mother stops drinking with her family. Takes the L to my apartment for an afternoon, sits against pillows propped on my bed, as though I am tucking her in. Small among the blankets, she says, *We can't keep doing this*, and I tell her I agree.

Later, my mother resumes drinking with her family. For my birthday she frames my preferred version of the photo, the one she fears may seem to be all about her: the way she laughs into the camera, as above her head I meet my sister's eyes. I keep the photo sometimes on my dresser, but other times under the bed. You tell me you love this picture. It's true we look so happy. I wonder, do you notice that it's gone? The times I flip it on its face?

Cinnamon Baseball Coyote

In the middle of a fight, when she is ten and Grace is six, Helen writes *I hate my sister* and puts the piece of paper in her desk. Three months later Grace finds it, while Helen is taking a shower. So then Helen with her wet hair wrapped up in a towel is saying: I wrote it a long time ago, Grace, and why were you looking in my desk? Their father, intervening, has been frowning. He says, Are you saying you forgot you had this, Helen? Grace is crying excessively, wiping her tears and nose on the pink sleeve of one bent arm. Helen says, I knew I had it, but I don't mean it anymore. I only kept it because I meant it *once*.

In their home there is a no-hitting rule, observed without exception—but their mother's sister could not possibly know it. This is why Helen, in the back seat of Aunt Eileen's car, on the Pennsylvania interstate, reacts with startling, thrilling physical violence to Evan's singing. One flat palm slapped across his upper arm, she says, Stop it, that is not a real song, you are making that up, be quiet.

Age one: impossible to remember. Their parents have Helen, and on her first birthday put her in a blue dress with smocking around the ribs and chest. There is a picture of it, framed, and they keep it hanging in the stairwell. In high school Evan smashes the picture frame running down the stairs. Slices open his elbow, bleeds on their carpet, gets six stitches. One Christmas Eve, in college, Grace is dressed for dinner and, descending, pauses on the stairs. She says, unprompted, I do like this picture, Helen, but I feel like there are better baby photos of you.

Evan is born. I am a sister now, joyful Helen tells the neighbors, famously.

Grace is born. Evan, age two, tells their father, Now I have two of these.

On the one day of winter break when it snows, Grace says with a small nose-wrinkle of distaste, These two are the artsy ones in this family, not me. Helen feels annoyed but Evan is fine. He just laughs and opens the fridge and looks around for the milk, saying, We actually think Grace could be an actress, if she tried. Helen says, I disagree, she's too purposely not caring. Grace says, How dare you, I was great that time you made me be your Peter Pan, remember how convincingly I cried? Grace's squash team friend is there—I'll have you know I wept, Grace tells her. The squash friend sips her glass of water and says, I've never been artistic myself, but of course I have to admire it. Grace says, Not me, I just like hitting things with my squash racquet. And she thumps one palm down hard on the countertop, which makes the nearby toaster give off a tinny, wild shudder.

Their parents meet just after college, in a bar, and it's raining. Later, their mother gives up her career to be at home with them. In middle school, Grace becomes incredible at squash. Of the three of us, says Evan over sushi one night in New York, Helen is most doomed.

Evan's plan is to not make the kind of mistakes Helen makes.

Pick yourself up, says her father, gently.

Helen cannot sleep all night and calls out sick from the coffee shop. This is not what people do, says her mother. What people do is, they go to work.

They try to remember an alphabet book they loved as children. S is for Serious. T is maybe for Timid, but they are not certain. Evan is trying to find the Yankees game on television. T is for Tearful, he guesses. Grace, flung out on the sofa, is wearing one of their mother's old college sweatshirts. She elaborates: T is for Tearful, like Helen is.

They're in high school when their dog gets old and dies. Her gums turn very pale and her small heart races, visibly beating under the skin. They and their parents take her to the vet, where they sit around her on the floor and stroke her until she falls asleep. The part of her Evan can reach is the small, warm armpit. They leave before she has the injection that will euthanize her. This is what the vet recommends they do.

The ground is too cold to dig into. For now their parents put their dog's ashes on a shelf, next to their mother's lightweight spring sweaters.

Evan, in elementary school, often tries to get a look at the top of his head. He thinks if he looks up quickly enough, he'll catch a glimpse. He stands in the family room and tips back his head, repeatedly.

Grace is uninterested in attending the play, so while Helen and Evan are getting ready she is on the couch watching television, eating smashed avocado on toast. Helen likes being inside the apartment with the two of them at this time of night, when it's cold out. Likes the way the windows in the building opposite come up in a cold gleam, and the sky turns. Evan is upstairs, looking for a tie. Helen is in the kitchen, ready, drinking a glass of water, liking the sound his soft footsteps make overhead.

When they first get their dog they are children, and argue incessantly about what to name her. Grace says, I am going to pull your hair. Evan says, I hate you both. In the end, the name is a kind of mash-up of their disparate suggestions.

College ice-breaker: My name is Helen and a fun fact about me is, my dog was named Cinnamon Baseball Coyote.

Years later Grace will sometimes say that if she could be reunited with anyone in the next life, it would be Cinnamon. Helen finds this vaguely insulting, and actually, so does Evan. We're your *siblings* he'll say to Grace, any time this comes up. I *know* that, Grace tells him, matching his tone. I'm *aware*.

They are children, and their father takes them with their Christmas present racquets to learn the game of squash. From the front seat, turning off the engine, he says, You all are going to really like this. Helen presses her face to the glass of one window: snow circles from the white sky, accumulates on the asphalt in a fine intricate layer, like pale moss. Under his breath, Evan is singing a made-up song. Grace says, Fine. But if I *don't* love this, Dad? I am not ever forgiving you, ever. Actually I'm not ever forgiving any of you. (So then Evan makes the next verse of his song

go: Don't blame me, don't blame me. And Helen says to
Evan: *Stop.*)

Years later, Evan will tell the story and laugh. Imagine
blaming me and Helen, he'll say to Grace, shaking his head,
and their mother will say, Imagine blaming your *father*, for
taking you out to play a game. Grace says, Well it worked
out fine. I did like squash. Everything turned out exactly
right. So Evan says, I'm happy for you Grace, it sounds
like you got some closure. And he winks conspiratorially
at Helen, who rolls her eyes and looks away.

The Goldfish in the Pond at the Community Garden

In the years I lived in that neighborhood, when I was twenty-seven and later twenty-eight, I visited the goldfish daily.

I didn't want people to know—it was my one secret thing. I had this friend in the neighborhood. He asked me once, at a party, if I had ever seen the fish, and I lied beautifully. I said, I didn't even know there *was* a community garden. What intersection?

After that, I always brought a book to the garden in case I encountered my friend. If I saw him, I imagined, I would turn the pages like I hadn't even noticed the fish, a flawless performance. I had a lie ready: *This is my first time here.* I felt there might be something between me and this man, but I was unwilling to lose the privacy of my daily ritual— even for him.

One day my friend called about a museum exhibit. He described dozens of perfect miniature staircases, spiraling up and up. I said I wanted to see the exhibit. My friend said, Where are you now?

In fact I had been on the brink of entering the garden. I'm nowhere, I told him. I mean, I'm at home. I agreed I would meet him, but I allowed myself a few minutes with the fish. Their scaly forms glinted, their pinwheel fins twirled against the water.

I was descending into the subway when I heard my phone again. The museum was closing, my friend said, but he had extracted a promise from admissions that we could go first thing tomorrow. This struck me as no great feat—tomorrow was Saturday, the museum was always open. Let's go up the Empire State Building, I heard myself say.

I'll meet you there, he told me. Some part of me wanted to go alone, perhaps—but now I had invited him.

Was it an accident I rode the subway too far? I ended up in Queens. I got off the subway and stood on the open-air platform. I imagined myself on the correct strand of the multiverse, arriving at the top of the Empire State Building winded and happy, the sky soft and red, the city's architecture shining in every direction, my friend raising his hand to wave.

Instead, I called him from the platform. I'm so sorry, I said. He told me, Stay where you are. I know that neighborhood. I could take you to this place with amazing fish tacos.

I thought of my goldfish turning in their pond. Okay, I said, tentatively.

I waited. I prowled through this neighborhood where I had never been. I enjoyed the sensation of being pursued from one borough into another entirely. When I happened upon a community garden, I slipped inside. It was lush and dark. No pond. An abstract sculpture hulked in one corner, and I put my hand against one of its planes, a sensation like placing my hand on a person's waist. I imagined running into someone I knew: *This is my first time here,* I would say, and it would be true. *What brings me to the neighborhood? I'm meeting someone for tacos.*

It grew darker, and the moment passed when he should have been calling to say he was close. I reached into my pocket to text him, and I found nothing. I put my hands into my other pockets. I rooted in my bag. I was surprised by the needle of dread I experienced, the sense that something grave was transpiring. I stopped a stranger on the sidewalk, through the garden's chain-link fence. I asked her to call my number, but: nothing.

Sorry honey, said the stranger as she continued on. My fingers clung to the lattice.

I retraced my steps—one block, another. My eyes scanned the pavement. I had the sense an essential window was closing, my fate slipping from me. Is it possible I was relieved? The lowering sun cast one side of the street in shadow, the other in honeyed light. The wind blew an empty paper cup across my path. Then I came around the corner and walked straight into my friend. He smelled like some familiar kind of flower, like sweat, and the subway. I held on to his arm. I felt like I could kiss him, or was it that he wanted to kiss me? I lost my phone, I said. I would never have found you.

He reached into his pocket, and the phone was in his hand. He'd stepped off the train, he said, and it was on the platform—his own name lighting up the screen. So then we went to eat our tacos, holding on to each other, certain we were the objects of some divine act. Across the table, we looked at each other with giddy alarm. It was uncanny. We kept laughing. For years afterward, this was our favorite anecdote to tell about ourselves to other people. It made everything foretold and essential that would come to pass between us: connection, love, marriage. The apartment we shared, the trip we took to Ireland, our walks we took on weekends through New York, the restaurant that was our favorite where they had this perfect chocolate cake.

I liked the sense of gravity that came over people when we told this story. I liked his hand holding on to mine with the force of fate as we spoke. It made it seem impossible we had made a mistake.

Then one day we were alone when he said: Imagine if we *had* made it to the exhibit at MoMA that day. No Queens, no tacos, your phone never went missing. Instead: Picasso, Calder, *Starry Night*. Dalí's clocks. The angularity of all the glass. We'd have sat in the sculpture garden as day became night, and it would have been a different story entirely.

We were sitting by the pond, watching the coppery fish twist and preen in the light. I closed my book and held it up to block the sun so I could look at him directly. Something in his facial expression unsettled me: his certainty. I said, I always remember the exhibit being at the Cooper Hewitt. I really could have sworn.

He frowned and said it wasn't the Cooper Hewitt though.

I'm certain that it was, I said.

He said I was certainly wrong. He said, I think you're misremembering.

● ● ●

This is why I didn't want to come here with you, I was on the verge of saying, but instead I told him: I would never misremember. I am excellent with details. It felt like the garden might wither around us as we looked at each other, our stories diverging. For a moment I felt alone, but then the fish were rising to the surface. They pierced the water in a clear shining mass and opened their small mouths. *It was the Cooper Hewitt*, they said to me. *It was. It was. It was.*

At the Time

— — —

At the time I was living in Minnesota, or maybe New York. Liz and I were engaged and sharing a light-filled apartment with beautiful tall windows, unless, by then, we weren't. I was twenty-seven unless twenty-eight. My subsequent girlfriend, Annie, expressed anger that I could not ever remember the chronology of how things unfolded, unless really she was angry that I loaded the dishwasher haphazardly and our drinking glasses kept cracking because of it. The glasses were patterned with small blue squares, unless they were patterned with red ones. The glasses were Annie's, unless they were Liz's and Annie wanted them all thrown away. I wanted to throw them away except that I wanted to keep them. I hated to throw things away except that I loved it, the wild unspooling reckless release. Goodbye, unless please stay. Harbor, unless don't. The windows in the apartment Liz and I shared cast warm areas of light across our floors and our bed and the kitchen appliances, except when it rained. We could see Washington Square Park through our small bathroom window, unless our apartment was in Minnesota. The reason is obvious or maybe it isn't: The Midwestern snow made the glass fog, unless it was just that we both closed our eyes. We cooked dinner unless it was takeout: Thai food, unless sushi. We cleaned unless we forgot. We got along famously except when we didn't, and slept in the same bed except when awake in the same bed. We ended things when she went back to Minnesota, or else when things ended I finally moved to New York. She kept the ring, unless I did. I look at it every day, unless I can't stand to think of it at all. I married Liz subsequent to being engaged to her, except only in the sense that I played out in my mind how that would have been if I'd actually done it. And Annie and I ended things when I broke the last of the drinking glasses, unless it was when I said I forgot the chronology of whether I dated her before or after Liz. What do you mean? Annie said, unless she said nothing and looked like she hated me. I said, It's just what I feel, or else what I said was, I know it's impossible. We had a catastrophic fight at this point, bitter and noisy, except for the critical juncture when we were just quiet, both of us breathing. I held her, unless I didn't. I told her to leave except she left on her own. I smashed up the drinking glasses out in the street, except that I lined them all up in the window, like chessmen, precisely, and with a kind of permanence. Afterward, I liked to watch the light play in the lines where they had fissured, unless the sun went down or I was doing something else that made me look the other way. There were twelve glasses altogether unless there were nine or five or two. I regarded them while making breakfast, unless I was late to work and stopping for a pastry on my way instead. At the coffee shop near work unless the one by my apartment. In the East Village, unless in St. Paul. I miss Minnesota except when I don't and I regret New York always, unless never. I would change plenty of things except that I wouldn't, and when I think about it that way there is no *what if*, there is no *then what*, there is only what I chose and did not choose, so many open doors evaporating all around me: one after another after another after another.

Aren't We Lucky

— — —

When he meets her at the airport, Emma's father says: *We are trapped in a problem of our own making. This was supposed to be done four weeks ago. The hammering is endless.*

At home he carries her suitcase upstairs, though it isn't so heavy she can't bring it up herself. Emma hovers in the doorway to the family room, where Nora is watching television. *Hi*, says Nora, and pats the couch beside her.

Sun glares in the windows, hammers pound overhead. Their parents are having the master bathroom gutted and refitted, though it is hard to understand exactly what will be improved by this. When Emma goes up to change her clothes, Nora follows. She lies across Emma's bed and says, *Mom is melting down. You would think something much worse had happened than back-ordered shower tile. You would think that you or I had cancer.*

There is a momentary cessation of noise in which they can hear the scrape of keys downstairs, and then their mother's voice. *I told her we're going to yoga,* Nora is saying, lifting herself onto her elbows. *She needs to calm herself— you're coming, too. I assume you need some calming down yourself.*

They go to Restorative Flow at a studio in town. In the parking lot Nora asks their mother, *Should we tell the class that it's your birthday? Maybe we can do a salutation to your sixties.*

Their mother says, *I'm not sure that's necessary,* Nora, and she points her keys at the car, which emits the cryptic shuttering of its locks. In class, she tells the woman on the next mat, someone she knows, *These are my daughters,* and Nora does a little wave. *You all look just the same,* says the woman, and her eyes move from one of them to the other to the other. Nora and Emma are used to this, being twins. *You look just like each other: you look just like your mother.*

The yoga teacher begins class by inquiring what everyone is looking for today, be it physical or spiritual or both. Nora offers that she feels shoulder tension as well as existential horror, and their mother gives her a sidelong look. Emma says nothing. Their mother says, *My intention for today is, when I get home, not to yell at the contractor,* and she delivers this remark in such a perfect, mostly-joking tone that the other women laugh appreciatively. Later, driving home, their mother observes: *There is nothing worse than a democratic yoga class, so much wasted time. Everyone going around saying what they want, I really hate that.*

Their mother has long held the opinion that Emma and Nora overemphasize their personal wants and feelings: *I didn't have the luxury at your age*, she'll often tell them. Then Nora will say, *Okay but now you live in a beach house, so I guess it all worked out.*

At home, cold wind blows over the driveway. Nora links her arm with Emma's and says, *I'm freezing, I'm so freezing.* In front of the garage several trucks are parked together, one with its passenger-side door gaping open. Beneath the deck that juts out from their parents' bedroom, a dumpster lies in wait: splintered boards stick up from it at jarring angles, like the limbs of something being resurrected horribly. It makes Emma feel strange, she looks away, as Nora says, *When I got here this morning, they were ripping up floor-boards and throwing them directly off the balcony. It was amazing.*

Inside the house, the hammers are deafening. In spite of the temperature, their father has retreated to the porch, where he sits reading in a fleece jacket Emma's never seen, something he must have bought since she left. *Hi*, says

Nora. *What are you reading?* Their mother is on her way upstairs, moving quickly toward the source of the hammering. She says to no one in particular, *I am at the end of my rope here.*

Emma goes to the kitchen to wash her hands. In the sink the dishes flinch, unified, with each percussive jolt overhead. She's turning to go upstairs and shower when a chunk of ceramic fixture tumbles past the window and crashes in the dumpster. *Jesus*, says Emma, as Nora bounds in from the porch. *Did it happen again?* Nora wants to know. *It sounded enormous. Did you see?*

Yeah, says Emma, and she feels her pulse fluttering, trying to slow. *That was awful.* Nora makes a clucking noise of sympathy, and the two of them embrace, a small joke, like they've survived something together.

Upstairs, turning on the shower, Emma notes a marbled wedge of men's soap, a pink razor, a murky facial serum, expensive and all-natural in a brown glass jar: her parents have been using this bathroom during the construction. They have made themselves comfortable; they had not been expecting her home soon. She looks at herself in the mirror, her hair falling over her shoulders as she untwists it from its clip, the rise and fall of her breathing. Her reflection seems to return her gaze as if missing some key detail: *Didn't you just move away? What are you doing here?*

To step into the shower is hot and soothing. Steam films over the glass and glows in the warm bathroom light, like something supernatural and encroaching. Emma uses some of her mother's shampoo though the bottle is nearly empty, and it makes her hair smell herbal, like strong tea. When she turns off the tap, the hammers are quiet again: she can hear footsteps coming up the stairs, and then her mother's voice down the hall, like gathering clouds. Wrapped in a towel, Emma cracks the bathroom door as Nora arrives at the landing, and they both mime freezing in their tracks. Then Nora puts a hand to her ear, and her face opens into a smile that wavers between delight and mortification.

This is not the timetable we agreed on, Greg, their mother is saying, *And I'm tired of repeating that.*

Nora says, softly, *You never listen, Greg. Use your ears, sir.*

Emma presses her lips together to hold in a laugh. *Although*, Nora continues, *It's not actually funny. She's being very entitled. Not a good day for Greg.* She adds darkly, as she goes into her room: *I would say I have lost the restorative flow, have you?* But she closes her door before Emma can answer.

Downstairs, sun through the window makes four bright squares across the countertops. Their father makes them all a late lunch of chicken salad on toast. Their mother joins them, still wearing her sleeveless yoga tank top, which shows the soft skin of her shoulders. Nora lifts the bread from her sandwich, as if preparing to clean the entrails from something she has personally killed. She begins to grind pepper over the exposed meat—but then the hammering recommences and she pauses, holding the pepper grinder with gentle authority, a picture of tolerant forbearance, like someone in a portrait bearing a scepter. Her hand clasps the curvature of the wood.

I'm going insane, says their mother, looking at the ceiling. She turns the tap on the sink and begins to wash her hands. *Mom*, says Nora, *No one here has cancer, yes? So I think you're actually okay.* Emma sees something ominous flicker in their mother's features, but Nora doesn't notice as she turns and turns the pepper grinder's head—a manic, provocative sound. Their mother's nostrils dilate, her mouth makes a little expression of derision, like she's affirming to herself she'll give this remark no actual consideration.

Thank you Nora, says their mother, *That's a very good point*. Another hunk of ceramic hurtles past the window and hits the dumpster with a thud.

Emma flinches, she has the breathless, potent sense of being pursued. But Nora is unfazed: *You know that could have hit one of us when you think about it*, she says, gesturing out the window, breezy and knowledgeable as their father might have sounded once, making some conceptual explanation to them as children: the rules of baseball, the virtues of capitalism, the phases of the moon. Nora says, *Scary, right?* She widens her eyes for emphasis.

Nora, says their mother in her most clipped, efficient tone. *We're indoors. It could not possibly have hit any of us.* She reaches to move a strand of Nora's hair back into place, as if Nora has some piece of inner machinery short-circuiting. But Nora can't be stopped: *Okay but if we were outside,* she says, *then it could have hit any of us. Like let's have some perspective. We're so lucky. Everything's great when you think about it that way.*

Their father says, *When you think about not being hit by a flying sink?*

Emma feels horrified laughter rising in her chest. *Walk me through this*, their mother is saying, *Where are we all standing in this hypothetical? Are we inside the dumpster?* To prove her point she looks out the window at where the sink has crash-landed, well within the bounds of the massive receptacle. Nora shrugs, *sure*, and their mother looks triumphant. *Well I can't think why we would ever do that, but you should of course feel free to enlighten me.*

At this, Nora meets Emma's eye, and Emma feels herself go still, instinctive as a deer or a rabbit.

Nora smiles. *Emma or I could have been in there processing our feelings about our childhood*, she says, with equal triumph in her voice. *I mean that dumpster is full of interesting stuff: it's the detritus of our dismantled family home, talk about symbolic.* Their father laughs as if in spite of himself. *Careful*, Emma says, because Nora's half-sandwich is starting to come apart in her grasp.

Nora, says their mother, drying her hands on a towel. *It's plumbing and floor tile, and you had a lovely childhood. I'm not sure what you'd need to process.*

Suddenly—precisely—their father deposits his plate in the sink. *I think I would like to take a nap*, he says. The hammering intensifies as if on cue, and in the orchestral swell, he stops to recalibrate, disoriented, seeming to reconcile the cacophony with the location of his bed. Their mother is saying, adamant, *I have no reason to think you or Emma would climb into a dumpster during active demolition.* She moves their father's plate into the dishwasher, then Emma's, then Nora's. She says, *You've never struck me as stupid.*

Nora shrugs again, and she takes Emma by the arm. *Let's take a walk*, she says brightly, and they leave their parents in the kitchen, amidst what sounds like the house beginning to fall in on itself.

They sit together on the porch, they lace their sneakers in the cold wind. *Those are nice*, Nora says, nodding at Emma's running shoes, and Emma says, *Nora I've had these for years.* Emma has the better memory between them—if pressed on a detail she can't recall, Nora will sometimes joke, *I blacked that out on purpose, don't remind me.* Emma watches her sister's fingers deftly pull the laces of her own shoes taut, first one, then the other, and it's like looking at her own hands, disembodied and outside herself.

Look who's home! says a familiar voice. They look up to see their next-door neighbor waving from the road, accompanied by her cocker spaniel whose improbable name is Steven. Nora goes to kneel on the pavement—*You sweet baby*, she says, and strokes the animal's ears. *Emma*, Mrs. Hoffman is saying, *I didn't think you'd be home for some time, how wonderful.* She means this: her broad smile is like light on water. In her blue windbreaker she reminds Emma of one of the candles the yoga teacher lit in class, to open everyone's throat chakras—she seems to flare comfortingly against the distant scenery of the beach. In the horseshoe bend of the cove, visible over Mrs. Hoffman's shoulder, Emma can see the ocean hurling wave after wave up onto the shore with unusual violence, all spit and foam where normally the protected water lies placid as an animal sleeping. She shivers. Mrs. Hoffman is asking, *What brings you two home?* She bestows her smile on each of them, and Emma says: *We're here for our mother's birthday.* Nora, loyal, only continues her professions of adoration to the dog—if she noticed Emma's evasion, she makes no sign of it.

It's their mother's birthday, yes, but their mother sets little store by birthdays. In reality they are here because Emma has made this abrupt choice to return, not just for a weekend but indefinitely. Nora is here only for a few days, out of solidarity—here to make distracting jokes, to take Emma's side in arguments, to intercept comments like, *Not everyone has the option to just come back to their parents, you know. Not everyone is so lucky.* But Mrs. Hoffman senses nothing amiss. She says, warmly: *Aren't you both wonderful to come home. And you traveled so far, Emma! I hope you have something planned to celebrate your mother— something really fun.*

Oh, says Nora, *Do we ever. We are pulling out all the stops. She won't know what hit her.*

Emma suppresses a laugh, because actually their mother has laid out firm and inviolable parameters for the birthday: they will go to dinner, there will be no candle. But Mrs. Hoffman is a birthday person, someone who cries at happy news, the sort of mother who still signs her grown children's names in holiday cards. *Sentimental*, their mother calls her, not unkindly but categorically, as if sentimental people are another species, unfathomable, equipped in ways that are interesting to think about and yet, for one's own purposes, functionally pointless.

Mrs. Hoffman makes a little movement of her chin and says, *How's all that, by the way*—because even from the road, the sound of hammering reaches them.

Nora raises her eyebrows to imply unspeakable mayhem, as a rain of pried-up floor tile falls from the balcony, raising dust from the point in the dumpster that swallows them. She says, *My suggestion to you is to ask our parents minimally about all that. You don't want to know.*

Mrs. Hoffman makes a soft noise of sympathy, and they all share a laugh tinged with alarm. The wind gathers force around them, and now Emma's hair is blowing across her face, like something she'll have to fight to escape. But Nora is already unwinding a hair tie from her wrist for Emma, another for herself. Emma was always the more conscientious sister when they were children, yet Nora has turned out to be the one prepared for living: good at talking to neighbors without timidity, equipped at key moments with necessities like hair ties.

You're perfect, you're so perfect, Nora is saying to the upturned, admiring face of Steven the dog.

When they say goodbye to Mrs. Hoffman, they follow the long road to the beach. Small birds in the sand flee their approach. With their heads lowered in the wind, it's difficult to hear, and this could be the reason Nora doesn't ask Emma what she plans to do next in her life, or why she quit the teaching job, or the reason she's come back when she had been so happy to leave—when only two months ago she was hugging Nora at the airport, saying: *You'll have to come visit me, okay? I won't be back any time soon.* But Nora doesn't ask, and Emma can't see how to start explaining, so they walk the beach in uncertain silence with their arms linked. Finally Nora says into the wind: *Such hospitable weather, you must be so happy you've come home!*

When they return, the trucks have cleared from the driveway. Inside, the quiet house has the eerie, private quality of an abandoned city. Nora throws herself on the couch, and as Emma joins her she catches sight of their mother, crossing the backyard—her beige jacket a specter in the lowering dusk. Wind flusters the landscape, leaves shudder on the trees, and their mother lifts her chin against the cold. She hasn't noticed her daughters through the window. If she did, Emma imagines the familiar scene would perturb her: Nora and Emma sprawled before the television, like they might have sat when they were five years old, nine, twelve, sixteen, two college students home on break. When Nora puts her head on Emma's shoulder, they are a closed circuit, their posture rippling with resonance across years, a resonance that might affirm, if their mother noticed them, her suspicion that the material ease of their lives has prevented them from growing up enough: Nora with her wise remarks and the tattoo their parents consider a profound error of judgment. Emma home from her thwarted adventure, the family gathered to receive her back in her failure to fulfill her own plans.

Perhaps Emma is imagining this. Maybe she's only real-locating, to her mother, her own self-criticism—maybe sitting again on this couch so soon after leaving has disoriented her, like she's slipping through years, losing count of her own age, becoming a child again: vulnerable and extreme. It's just that she feels disappointing, like she has done so little with what she's been given. *Look how much you have*, their mother was always saying to them—standing at the marble-topped kitchen island, for example, with a movement of her hand that seemed to reduce the whole room to a sad joke, like it was deflating around them. *So many people don't have enough, and you have all of this.* Once, Nora had asked: *Do you wish we didn't live here?* They were maybe fourteen, and Nora meant it, but their mother took the question for taunting. *You're not listening to me*, she said, and Emma saw Nora's confidence falter briefly as their mother turned to look out the window—averting her gaze as if from something gruesome.

What's up with you, Nora says now, switching on the tele-vision. *You look haunted. Did you see a ghost? Have the murdered bathroom fixtures come to avenge their deaths?*

She draws her knees to her chest, and on her ankle Emma can see the tattoo their parents openly disdain. She thinks of yoga class earlier today, the other women's eyes moving over the two of them, not unkindly but hungrily, apprais-ingly—weighing the in-the-flesh daughters against how their mother would have described them. Nora the smart aleck who never knows when to stop talking. Nora who came home after their freshman year at college with the hated tattoo. *It's the astrological symbol for Cancer actu-ally*, Nora said, and their mother did not mince her words: *What it looks like is the number 69.* As if this were a mat-ter of perspective, Nora responded blithely, *Maybe to you.* That week in yoga class their mother might have said, *My intention today is, I'll just let her be stupid if she wants to be.* But Nora has turned out fine: she lives with her boy-friend, she's recently been promoted, she goes on weekends away with her various friend groups—so various their par-ents have trouble remembering who she's with, and where. Meanwhile Emma has only a cloudy sense of not meeting expectations. Her unexplained decision to come home must have occasioned a similar pronouncement in this loose cir-cle of yoga-class confidantes, something more for everyone to laugh at in rueful support: *I'll just let her be stupid if it's what she wants. Not that I had the option at her age.*

But today, in the calm conviviality before class, amidst all the women unfurling their mats and murmuring greetings, Emma had felt a passing illusion that sheer proximity to her sister, so impossible to throw off balance, might protect her—as if Nora's presence might speak for both of them, write over anyone's preconceived sense of them. Nora made a quip, she stretched her legs out on the yoga mat and people laughed. The familiar tattoo peeked from the ankle of her yoga pants. Emma stretched her legs out the same way and experienced something like ease, a willingness to let everyone look at her. She closed her eyes.

What are we watching?

Again Emma notices the urgent response of her own pulse. *Dad*, says Nora, turning to where he stands in the doorway, *You just scared the shit out of us*. Their father is apologetic, but Nora is already talking over him, answering his question: *We're watching* Sex and the City *of course*, she says, although they aren't—it's an old joke between them, a thing they said as teenagers when they wanted the TV to themselves. *Ah*, their father would always say, and drift off, carefully. Even now he seems prepared to leave, but Nora says, *I'm kidding, we're not watching anything, we're flipping through our options. We're blissfully idle.* Concern crosses their father's face, and it seems he may say something fatherly, like, *Let's come up with something productive you can do then*. But in the pause before he speaks, the bright light and frantic noise of the television go dark and silent, like a house where the power has been cut.

In the sudden quiet, it feels not unlike the room has been dropped underwater.

Did you do that Emma? says Nora, though she is the one holding the remote. Her eyes glimmer with intrigue as she reaches to grip Emma's wrist. *Is the television haunted?*

By whom? says their father, clearly against his better judgment.

The ghosts of the master bathroom, presumably, says Nora. *They're enraged by the general disturbance.* She hands their father the remote, as if he might know what to do, but he only turns it over in his hands. *Well*, he says and sets the remote back on the coffee table, at which point the television comes back to life, in a burst of light and canned fragmentary laughter.

What the fuck, says Nora, thrilled.

Then, in the window, Emma sees something move—but no, it's only the reflection of Nora, reaching over to pick a bit of lint from Emma's sweater. Still, even as Nora's fingers brush along her arm, Emma is left with a curious intuition of some creature scaling the exterior of the house—up to the dark cave of the gutted bathroom.

She pictures the bathroom's arteries of wire, its open walls and decaying wood, and something at the window trying to come in.

Maybe this is why, when she and Nora go up to change for the birthday dinner, Emma feels strange, heady gratitude for the contrast of their own intact bathroom. Like the bright organization of this room is a last defense against some growing pandemonium beyond. At the mirror she slides bobby pins into her hair while privately appreciating the clean lines of grout between the tiles, the long seal of the shower door, the overhead light's secure glow emanating into the hall. Nora sits filing her nails on the edge of the tub. *Let's hope*, she says, *that everyone behaves tonight. If not, we'll run away from home.*

In the mirror, her reflection winks at Emma's. *Just kidding*, her reflection says. *We're too old for that. There is nowhere to run.*

When Emma goes downstairs, her scarf in her hand, it slinks on the stairs beside her. *I'm right behind you*, says Nora, who is still choosing which earrings to wear. In the kitchen Emma finds their mother in a dress gray and velvet as water, the overhead lamp reducing her to silhouette, her back to Emma at the sink. Her hands turn over a toothy piece of metal kitchen equipment under the faucet, and Emma says, *What is that*, but her voice isn't audible over the water in the drain. And for a moment she is a ghost. She is trying to speak across dimensions, trying to communicate. The dishes accumulate, warm and clean, and the idea of plates and cutlery reaches Emma from a distant past, comforting words in a language she once knew, an aspect of her onetime terrestrial existence she can only dimly try not to forget. The orbs of wine glasses shine like pearls, and Emma's mother's face appears in profile again and again as she sets each one aside, as serious in her task as a child assigned a chore. Then Emma has the strange and ridiculous certainty that in another life they all knew each other, that Emma and Nora were the parents, that their parents were the children. Emma's eyes fall on her mother's outstretched arm, and it's like she can see through the silver velvet to her skin, and then down to her bones.

When her mother turns and switches on the light, she doesn't expect Emma behind her. Surprise escapes her as a gasp, an involuntary movement of her hand to her throat, and then the feeling seems to evolve inexorably toward some less certain emotion, like an occult energy let go from the box that has for years contained it. Her posture straightens as if at the bidding of some greater force, she seems to look down from a point high above, and Emma has a sense of suspense so heady she reaches to hold the kitchen counter. Her eyes are closed when she feels her mother embrace her. They stay this way, arms around each other. Their breath rises and falls, the velvet dress soft under Emma's hands. *Oh*, says Nora's voice from the doorway presently. *Are we having a moment of profound love?* She comes over and leans her head against Emma's back.

Their father's footsteps approach down the stairs and pause in the doorway, and their mother clears her throat. *All right*, she says, and straightens up, and touches Emma's elbow as if to dismiss her. She touches her own hair back into place, and Emma feels herself do the same. *Shall we?* says their father, looking at all of them fondly, uncertainly. *Yes*, says Nora, *Please. I'm unbelievably hungry, I'm barely keeping it together.*

They're in the garage before Emma realizes the scarf she held is gone. Nora makes her voice a parody of urgency: *Run Emma, there isn't time! A dinner reservation is at stake.* The garage door is barreling upward, their father is turning the shuddering ignition on the car, the headlights project Emma's shadow on the wall. *I'll be quick*, she says. When she moves out of the headlights, away from her family, it's as if she's disappearing.

In the extinguished kitchen, the shape of her scarf huddles darkly on the floor. She kneels to pick it up. Later, she will be unable to describe what she saw next, what it looked like that made it so clearly what it was. She simply looked up to see it falling. A person with her sister's face, her mother's face, her own face, the face they all three share. The ghost turns its head to look at her, the ghost reaches its hand out to her, the ghost is falling down a long-worn inevitable path. Emma runs.

At dinner, there will be silver balloons their father has arranged for in advance. There will be a candle, poised in a triangle of cake. Their mother will be studied in her dismissiveness even as delight sparkles for a moment in her voice. *I didn't need this*, she'll say—inhibited perhaps by the possibility of loving something that might slip from her. Later, at home, Emma will describe the ghost to Nora, who will listen, and gasp, and eventually say, just before they go to sleep, *I'm so fucking jealous Emma, I can't believe you saw through space and time.* Then she'll say, nodding toward their parents' door, *Let's not tell them.* She'll hover barefoot on the threshold of her room and say, *They won't believe us, right?* Dimly, before she shuts the door, Nora will hold her fingers to her lips. *Our secret*, she'll say. And she'll move into the darkness of her own room, as if transcending some fixed boundary.

In the morning they will all wake to the resumed drumbeat of the master bathroom's ongoing desolation.

The ghost will move from room to room—dislodged from whatever part of the house has, till now, been holding her.

The hammers will be like what she remembers of head-aches: sharp and final, familiar and merciless. Her hands will pass through every lock and window latch, through the keys waiting on the kitchen counter, through the well-made handle of every exterior door. Her fingers will gain no purchase, and she will feel a rising permanence, like she is fated to reach for doors in perpetuity until some reso-lution untethers her. She'll remember how it felt to have a pulse—how it would have leaped at the sight of the shape that falls down past the window, slams against the ground. Finally she will choose a door and wait there, flickering, attuned to the possibility of footsteps. Eventually someone will open this door, she reasons. At a certain point some-one will have to. And she will wonder, when it opens, will she leave.

Like a Cloud,
Lighter Than Air

After Christmas, as she tries to swim up from her sadness, things that have always seemed laughable to Helen
become comforting: Fate, for example. The possibility of
divine intervention.

Before this, she always put her faith in ambition, effort,
careful choices—things she was raised to believe in. Things
that may just be myths, the trappings of so many systems
at work. And at the coffee shop, this other barista, Rory, is
going through a weird time, too, which seems to affirm that
life is not like what Helen thought. One day the two of them
unload the dishwasher together in a warm cloud of steam,
lifting mugs one by one from the rack. Rory explains that
she's been saving for an appointment with a $200-dollar-
an-hour psychic, in an effort to get some perspective.
Sometimes, says Rory, you just have to get beyond yourself,
you know? The psychic's credentials include predicting a

well-known helicopter crash Helen's never heard of. It was a big deal at the time, Rory tells her.

Winter break is ending: Evan is back at college, rehearsing for the play, and Grace has one more week at home. Their father says to Helen, Maybe you'd feel better if you got some exercise. You and your sister could play a round of squash. Grace is sitting on the kitchen counter, scrolling on her phone, wearing athletic shorts and one of Helen's sweaters. She says, pointedly: I can make my own plans, thank you Dad.

Helen's behavior strikes their mother as an overreaction. Life is change, she tells Helen one afternoon. Analyzing so much can't change what's already happened to you. And Helen says, Do you think I don't know that? That, obviously, is the whole problem right now.

That afternoon, Helen and her mother wrap up in scarves and winter coats and go walking. Across town to the East River, then south and further south. Her mother moves her gloved hand in circles on Helen's back. This fanatic grief—like a baby, Helen thinks, mortified and grateful. *The mother walks her daughter up and down the East River while she cries and cries.*

That night, on the internet, Helen identifies a more afford-able point of divine access than Rory's: a tarot reader working out of an occult bookstore in Bushwick. The tarot reader has many effusive Yelp reviews. According to her website, a decade of formal dance training preceded her spiritual awakening. In her photograph, she has beautiful, intricately tattooed hands: scarlet, yellow, blue, and violet.

Grace can hardly believe it. Welcome to the New Age, she says, when Helen comes into the kitchen and explains, tentatively, that to feel better or get unstuck or whatever, she has just paid forty dollars via PayPal to reserve a reading. Their parents are out to dinner, and Helen and Grace eat pesto on pasta, leaning against the kitchen counter. Grace twirls spaghetti around her fork. She says, Does this mean you'll drink kale smoothies with me now? Since you're a hippie?

Evan finds it an impossibly funny development. On their group text, to which Grace has assigned the title *Siblings*, he sends them a string of laughing-crying emojis—then sends more a few hours later when, apparently, the whole thing hits him again with fresh hilarity. Their parents, however, are surprisingly nonplussed. Whatever will help, says their mother, putting restaurant leftovers in the fridge. Their father says, But do try to get some exercise, Helen, like I keep saying. Go for a run. It clears the mind.

That night Helen can't sleep at all. In the morning she calls out sick from the coffee shop and lies on the couch feeling foggy and pulverized. Eventually her mother, who has been running errands, comes home and unpacks farmers' market produce into the fridge. She says, This is not what people do in life, Helen. The way you're being is not how people are. Not everyone has the privilege of sitting on the couch being sad.

That night, her father takes her to dinner so they can talk, just the two of them. It's time to pick yourself up, he says over dessert. Please try to feel better. Helen is crying a little. These past few months have been like the crying saturation point of her life. He says: Is there something more that we can do to help you out here? Helen says she can't explain it, but lately she just feels so selfish, like a lot of trouble, like not a good person. She says he should please just hold her to a high standard going forward.

The candle between them on the tablecloth wavers. Her father regards her with a level, concerned expression and says, Okay, I can do that. Later, at home, brushing her teeth, Helen realizes with a fresh current of self-loathing how this sounded, maybe, like she blames him. Downstairs, Grace is asleep on the couch, so Helen texts Evan instead: *I think I just said something awful to Dad.* Evan texts back: *Can't talk now Helen, but I'm sure it's not actually a problem. Take it easy.*

That night, she can't sleep again. In the dark the memory comes to her of another dinner with her father: home from college, she tells him she's been turned down for a small grant she'd applied for from the university, to put on a play. People hate giving things to women, she'd said, and surprised herself by voicing this thought, which had been resurfacing in her mind for days like a curious recurring dream of thwartedness and limitation, a clear intuition unless it was an excuse, entitlement, failure to admit defeat—she couldn't tell. How could you tell your own failure from having been failed? She could only point out that her college had chosen a man, like last year and the year before. Anyway, her father was encouraging. He said, This isn't something your generation has to worry about, it's all on the upswing, I hire lots of women. And she had said to him, her temper leaping like a flame: You have no idea what you're talking about.

I think I'm not really a great person, she confides to the same co-worker, Rory, when they're on shift together later that week. She says, I think I do more harm than good. Or I expect more than I deserve. Rory laughs and says, I doubt it, dude, but I get it—sometimes I beat myself up, too. Wiping down the espresso machine, Rory says: I don't see you as a bad person, but it does seem like you're super, super upset. I hope it's not weird for me to say that. I know you don't really know me.

Rory suggests the two of them go out for dinner after they close up the coffee shop. She says they clearly both need to have fun, get out of their heads, try to feel better, just chill. She mentions a hip Asian Fusion place on the Lower East Side: The food is so fucking good you will die, she tells Helen. It takes them forever to walk there from the F train, and they laugh, and gripe about how cold they are, and lower their heads against the wind. At dinner, Rory visibly annoys the waitstaff by ordering only an appetizer and eating it more slowly than it seems possible anyone has ever consumed a single pork bun. Listen Helen, she says, flagging the waiter for another glass of water, Here is what I do when *I'm* depressed: I write in my journal. I go to therapy. I get serious about the gym. I read. I watch funny videos on the internet. I will send you my list of funny videos—it is an awesome fucking list, you'll be uplifted. You're not a bad person Helen, she says. You're sad. Or I don't know, angry? I mean of course you are, so am I, of course we're sad.

Helen is not prepared to absolve herself but promises to try the funny videos. Afterward, outside, they type their numbers in each other's phones, and then Rory calls an Uber—she's been crashing with friends, she explains, ever since moving out of her stupid ex's place last month. And suddenly Helen is explaining about Catherine. My oldest friend, she hears herself saying. We had this fight, we stopped speaking. The thing is, I probably deserve this. I expect too much. I hold people to a ridiculous standard. Lately it's like I'm seeing myself clearly for the first time in my life.

Rory crosses her arms, the wind blows her hair across her face. She says, I don't know Helen, this girl sounds like a flake. You really don't need that dragging you down. Give me your phone. We could block her number. Do you want to?

Once, in high school, Helen directed Evan in the school play, opposite Catherine as his love interest. After rehearsals, driving home together down the quiet highway, Helen liked the three of them cocooned in the dark. Catherine beside her, cycling through radio stations for the songs she liked best, and Evan in the back seat, singing and commenting on her choices. You're so completely unoriginal, Catherine would tell him if he disliked what she played. You have so much to learn.

Ah, Catherine, Evan liked to joke, long after the play had ended. Catherine my lost love. Catherine who can really, really kiss.

Their parents are driving to Vermont to see Evan in his play next week, and they ask does Helen want to come? Grace can't, because of her squash tournament, and Helen considers lying that the coffee shop won't give her time off. Is that bad? she asks Grace, who's folding laundry on the couch, while Helen lies on the floor and looks up at the ceiling. The overhead lights form bright elastic orbs in her vision, as the laugh track from the television crests and ebbs and crests again. Well, she hears Grace saying, You're kind of flipping out in life, but Evan is like, thriving. So it makes sense to me that you would want to bail.

A little while later, without any real hope, Helen tries Catherine once more and gets the inevitable voicemail, serene and gracious. *This is Catherine, leave a message.* Grace says, getting up to make herself toast: This is all fairly shitty of Catherine, you have to admit.

People at the coffee shop misunderstand, and fair enough. I live here with my family, but I'm not from here, Helen explains to Rory, while they mop, respectively, around the tables and behind the counter. She says, My parents moved away to raise us, and recently they came back. She adds, affecting an ironic tone: I myself grew up in some nearby suburbs. Rory for her part is from a town near Minneapolis. She asks, over the hissing emissions of the milk steamer: But so Helen, where do you think of yourself as coming from, exactly?

That night, when she gets home from work, Helen finds Grace and her mother on the floor, sorting through a box that for some reason they never unpacked. Grace says, Look at these squash trophies I didn't even know were missing. Their mother shows them a number of gray scale snapshots from their father's childhood, and one or two from her own. She lays them one by one along the rug.

Their mother's mother died very young, when their mother was only two, and on a few occasions Helen's tried to ask: Don't you want to find out more about her? But their mother would rather not. She says it's easier not knowing. Now Helen holds a photo to the light and says, Mom, does it make you sad to think about her? Grace says, Let me see it, can I? Helen. Let me see. Their mother says, Be careful with your fingers on that, both of you, listen to me.

Helen can remember being a very young age. She remembers for example a dream from before Evan was born: she is tucked beneath her mother's arm, and the two of them make pancakes. After breakfast they leave home in search of her father, whom they locate playing in a kind of country-fair band. It seems to be an origin story. They are choosing out a father for their family: this one waves, and they bring him home. For a short time Helen really thought it went that way. First it was only she and her mother. Followed by the addition of a father, then Evan, then Grace. Finally Cinnamon the dog. She can remember her feeling of complete belief. She can remember telling her father: Before you, Dad, there was me.

On the afternoon of Helen's tarot reading, the temperature is unseasonably warm. Along the paving stones, in Union Square, dry brown leaves skitter and turn over in wind. As she descends into the subway station, Helen hears a father at street level say to his small children: No one ever listens to me. One of them responds: I listen, Dad, I listen. In the station, Helen tries to get the machine to read her MetroCard. She swipes it again, and again, and again.

She takes the L train across Manhattan, through its dark tunnel beneath the East River. Arriving in Brooklyn, she navigates blocks of mostly warehouses, following the map on her phone, its pulsating blue dot her guide. A bell over the front door rings when Helen enters the bookstore, and from a picture online she recognizes the tarot reader right away: leaning against a display of crystals, talking to a girl at the register, long hair pulled back from her face.

In the curtained-off area between Numerology and Past Lives—a space so small Helen has to shove her backpack under the table—the tarot reader lights a stick of incense, her dance training evident in the exquisite precision of her gestures.

It's up to you, she tells Helen, whether you want to channel a higher energy from your angels and guides, by turning up your palms, or more of a grounding energy by touching the tops of your knees. Hesitantly, Helen chooses: knees. The tarot reader shuffles the cards in the smoke from the incense, which billows in a thin plume between them. From a small bit of exploratory reading Helen has done, she knows this has something to do with dispersing old energy.

The reader says, I'd like to invite you to close your eyes. We'll just do a brief clearing meditation, to sort out some of the gunk. The last thing Helen sees is the tarot reader drawing a breath so deep her eyelids flutter. Then comes a pause, silent except for the ruffling of cards, soft and fluid like wings. Presently the tarot reader hazards that Helen has been learning some difficult karmic lessons lately. She says that she can sense this clearly—the spirit guides are telling her as much. The bell over the door to the bookstore jingles, as Helen's eyes fill up with tears. The tarot reader keeps hers closed, and listens.

You have to get rid of the clutter, is one thing she advises. Her expression is concerned and analytic. Clean house, she says. Throw things away. Let go of dead weight. This is an essential practice. If not, she says, you'll be looking at a spiritual situation sort of like this—and she shows Helen a card with a burning castle on it, and bereft-looking people falling out of it headfirst. But if you do clean house, she says—and then she stops, closes her eyes again, and lets out a soft, delighted laugh. Listening to this other plane, apparently. She says, They're saying you won't like the change at first, but later, you'll be so happy you did it. They're showing you to me as, like, a cloud: you are lighter than air.

On her way home from the reading, at the corner of 17th Street, Helen runs into Grace coming back from the racquet club. The wind runs down Park Avenue—it's dark now, colder, and Helen dips her face into the folds of her scarf. Grace lets her racquet case hit a lamppost, a trash can, a newspaper kiosk, and she says over her shoulder, Can we walk faster please?

Inside, upstairs, their parents are taking ornaments off the Christmas tree. Grace will not participate: I hate this part, she says, as their mother wraps a silver bell in newspaper, then a crystal bird with a chipped wing. Their father asks, gamely, How was the tarot reading? But Helen says, I'm not sure I'm prepared to discuss this, I think I need to think the whole thing over.

Upstairs, Helen says to Grace: Sometimes life is so extremely strange. Grace says, turning her face into her pillow, I'm sorry you feel that way.

That weekend, they drop Grace off at college on their way to Evan's play. Bye Helen, says Grace when they hug each other in the parking lot. I hope everything becomes the way you want. From the back seat, for the rest of the drive, Helen watches snow-crowned hills flash past the window. Cows stand, stoic and congregated, in fenced-in fields. By the time it's dark, her parents are arguing about why they were sure the play began at seven thirty, not seven. Whether this means they're going to be late, and whose fault this might be, and the consequences. Rory texts, *Pro tip: psychic says self-pity will only impede the activities of fate, haha.* Helen writes back, *You went?!* Rory says, *So much to tell you.*

In the play, Evan is charismatic, moving, wonderful. Helen is jealous, jealous, jealous. After the play they go to dinner, and after dinner is a cast party, and while their father signs the check, Evan says to Helen: If you want, you can come. The party will be at someone's off-campus apartment, and on their way they stop to buy a six-pack from a fluorescent-lit minimart. At the party, the dark-haired girl who's playing Viola keeps saying, Wow, Evan's *sister*, I totally see it!

She and Helen end up talking in the kitchen, and every time someone passes through, the girl says, Come over here and come meet Helen, Evan's sister, can't you see it? Look. As children, they were often mistaken for twins. No, their mother was always saying, Helen is small but Helen is older. In time Helen learned to preempt the inquiry: I'm Helen, she'd say, and our parents had me first. Then Evan would add, But I am just tall and could be taller in the end. That's just a true thing about boys.

Tell us something about baby-Evan, says the girl who plays Viola, hopefully, as she pries open another beer. Helen offers up a memory from elementary school: Evan finally learned to tie his shoes, and then he said, candidly, Now I know everything. Coming to stand in the doorway, Evan says, The part she's not telling you is where she said to me, You're stupid, you're so stupid. He says: Talk about a psychic wound.

Then, sort of wincing, he peels at the label on his beer. So Helen says, dismissive: He's acting, he's fucking with us. Which Evan concedes with a small grin, taking a long draw on his beer. But seriously, Helen says, It's true I'm trying to become someone better, someone kinder. I'm not always a good sister.

Evan says, irritable, Oh can't we stop with this already? Stop. No one thinks that you're so terrible. It's kind of indulgent to keep putting us all through this. But the castmate, Laura, says to Helen, You're braver than I am, I don't like to look at me too closely. She toasts Helen with her drink, but Evan is almost sneering—he says, You have to stop talking this way, you were, are, totally acceptable. The castmate says, High praise! and suddenly Helen can't stop laughing. She reaches to steady herself with a hand on the other girl's shoulder. Without me, she says, these past few weeks, my brother could not once remember the line where "savage jealousy sometimes savors nobly." So in a sense, I saved your play.

The girl starts laughing, too, but Evan says, Don't be an idiot Helen. Helen says, You don't be an idiot, I'm obviously kidding. The castmate looks between them and says,

Sibling rivalry, I love it, is it just the two of you? Helen says, No there's also Grace, but she's younger and an athlete. The castmate fishes for a corn chip from a nearby bowl— Oh right, she says, the tennis champion. No, says Helen, but Evan cuts in: Any time you say "athlete," Helen, you say it as if she were another species.

Helen says to the other girl, like this explains it: Grace has these arms that he and I will never have. She's very disciplined. But Evan pushes back the sleeve of his T-shirt— Speak for yourself, he says, and raises his eyebrows for the castmate's benefit.

When they leave the party Evan says he'll walk her to the inn. Good, says Helen, I don't know how to get there. Down the stairway, out into the yard, they pick their way over snowbanks, step out into the empty gutter of the clean, plowed street. Helen breathes cold air, feels the snow press underfoot, and then suddenly both their phones chime from their pockets: Grace. *Guess what, Catherine just followed me on Instagram.*

Evan shouts into the empty street, Catherine you bitch! Fucking brazen! I can't think of any greater offense ever perpetrated!

Helen is still looking at her phone. Don't make fun, she tells him vaguely.

Helen, he says, I'm finding the humor. Lighten the fuck up please.

They're saying good night on the steps of the inn when he remembers about her tarot reading. She says, I'll tell you in the morning. No Helen, he says gravely, If you've had interventions from the universe, I need to know about them now. She says, Shut up, good night, I'll see you at breakfast. Set your alarm, I don't want to wait around like last time.

Across the vacant lobby, she's halfway upstairs when her phone goes off again: *But I really want to know*, says Evan. She relents, stopping on the darkened staircase to respond. *For real: the future holds cleaning my room. Not kidding. This is my destiny. Haha.* She sends him a moon emoji, a crystal ball, some stars. He sends back more laughing-crying emojis, with tears flying off their faces.

Later that week, back in New York, she relates it all to Rory while they walk from the coffee shop to a bar nearby, in the blue light of early evening. Rory in turn details her experience with the psychic, sounding almost pleased: He said my ex and I are not optimally compatible—and I said to him, it's a bit fucking late for "optimal" okay? I mean at a certain point you love who you love.

Someone's dog, on a leash, gives them a bright, passing, anticipatory glance. Rory lights a cigarette and says, Fuck,

I'm so nostalgic sometimes Helen, I don't know if I could do what you're describing: throw out all my stuff.

Helen reaches into the pocket of her coat and finds her receipt from the mini-mart in Vermont. Look, she says, and crumples it experimentally, admiring the crushed feel of it in her hand before she abandons it to the depths of a green metal trash can at the corner of Eighteenth and Park.

Rory cackles appreciatively. She says, Do you feel lighter already?

Helen says, I feel uplifted. She raises her arms in the air, an unexpectedly beautiful sensation—as though she were afloat over lower Manhattan on a cold, dry wind.

Briefly

— — —

But why have I never mentioned Dublin, he wants to know. And the answer is something like: There is no explaining some things, no resolution to certain stories.

In general, I rarely talk about Dublin, as if by not referring to it I can keep what was good in the summer, divest myself of all the rest. But tonight my friend and I have left a party and now we're at a bar on Irving, a place whose moody light suggests possible communion and camaraderie, and something about how close we're sitting makes me think of Hallie Wolfe, so cuddly with all of us in Dublin. She'd drink one whiskey in the pub, then she'd be between your arm and ribcage: shorn hair soft beneath your chin, ear to your collarbone. Like she planned to be there for the rest of the evening. *I love you!* she'd coo, *You're my favorite, you're great*, into the space in the side of your neck.

You laughed and resigned yourself, no use resisting.

When was this, when were you in Ireland? my friend wants to know, like he's checking his math on me. And I'm feeling the fizzy eloquence of a few drinks, so I don't change the subject. I say, Eleven years ago, undergrad, a summer writing program—should we get another round? His hand is on the bar, just touching his near-empty drink, and he nods to the bartender, *another*, turns his attention back to me. I say that I met Hallie Wolfe for the first time too early in the morning on a bleary taxi ride from Dublin Airport. That she explained to me, in the back seat of the cab, that she was looking for someone on the trip who would assist her in dyeing her pink hair green. That she further explained she was going to an indie rock concert in Cork next weekend, that she was a sophomore at Stanford, that she preferred "Hallie" to her legal name, Patricia, and so on, etc., etc., etc.

The next night in the pub on Rathmines Road that would soon become our favorite, we drank a round of beers in the fragile glow of our nascent group dynamic—Hallie Wolfe, me, Clare, Lena, Sasha, Alice Doolan, James Gallagher, and so on, all of us, even the program director, Daniel Byrne—while Hallie explained how her mind had an anomaly, or was it an ability? *Synesthesia*. It made her see letters in association with color. It made her remember information to a remarkable degree, in vibrant shades of scarlet, orange, teal, etc. We were at once captivated and skeptical when she told us her given name, Patricia, was plain and drab and gray, but that "Hallie" was a pretty, inky melding of pink and deep magenta when the letters bled together inside the picture in her brain.

My friend seems almost to rearrange his sense of me as I say this, making space for the new slice of backstory, like moving furniture around a room. We've only been friends a few months but there's this easy rapport between us and I can tell he thinks he would have known, by now, the places I have lived my life. He raises his eyebrows and I circle a red cocktail straw around my drink and say, half-joking, that my own associations, however intense, don't map onto colors, shapes, or sounds—so it is not synesthesia, what I have, it is only vivid remembering. I say I looked it up to be sure, the same night Hallie said all this, on my laptop in the kitchen at 13 Devlin Road, an address I recall because I loved how deceivingly permanent it felt, like it would be our house forever, and because we vowed we'd meet again at our favorite pub just up the road in ten years' time—a date that has since come and gone, unobserved and without fanfare.

When I say this, my friend laughs like I am revealing something essential of myself to him, and I wonder if I've played a card I should be holding. He's a new friend and here still is the old uneasiness, first seeded after that summer in Dublin: fear of becoming too close too quickly.

On that first day, in our taxi, Hallie and I only passingly discussed her name. I shrank into my half of the back seat, tried to signal I was too tired for conversation, as the taxi sped along the flat gray motorway and Hallie wanted to know: What did I think about the news feed, and did I think it limited our ability, as a generation, to process other points of view? Did I not think the effects might be dangerous—having our subjective interpretations of events reinforced for us that way? In truth, it was something I had never thought of—the year was 2009, I was not yet twenty-one—so I just said, *I don't know*, and turned to stare out my window, quiet, as Hallie set upon the cab driver, asking: *Is Dublin known for any sort of wildlife?*

On my side of the car, I cringed, groused inwardly that this was a frankly embarrassing American question. While in Dublin, I spoke little in public. In an attempt at blending in, all of us on the trip appropriated a certain inquiring cadence, "the Irish up-question," we called it, not entirely precisely. I didn't want anyone to catch my accent, I hoped to be mistaken for belonging. I hated to be an American from a suburb outside New York City, which felt like coming from a place so neutral it was meaningless, a void in my identity that anyone might project anything upon. One night, at the pub, a stranger said to me: *You have a very nervous disposition, don't you?* Later he insisted on knowing where each of us was from, and to me he said: *Ah. You've been well taken care of.*

But when Hallie asked her wildlife question, the cab driver in his cotton-candy sweater said: Foxes. Dublin was full of them. They'd move like gusts of wind into the road at night, as if from nowhere. So Hallie had not asked a silly question, and days later, it would prove useful: we determined a fox had to be what Alice Doolan heard at Devlin Road, the day she came running from the third floor to the kitchen, where I was making a sandwich with the back doors open on the concrete garden with its clothesline and its view of chimneys, when she burst in distraught, demanding to know, *Are you all right? Were you just shouting?*

The scream of a fox would prove to be an eerie, wretched cry, approximating that of a human female, only wordless. It was only our first week in Dublin, and we would listen all summer for the sound.

On the same night Hallie Wolfe explained synesthesia to us in the pub, James Gallagher described for us a story he was writing. It was really several stories stacked inside each other, like nesting bowls, he said. The further you read, the more uncertain you became, the more garbled and rough and slapdash the language, the more inscrutable the grip on reality and train of thought, the more you lost the plot. I'm reaching for my whiskey now, wondering if my friend might think, from all I've said about Hallie Wolfe, that she is at the center of this story with no resolution, when actually it's James Gallagher. This is part of the irresolution:

I am always looking at the periphery of this story, away from the uncomfortable center. Away from James Gallagher, tall and wiry with his anxious eyes, his hand reaching to hold on to my arm. Away from how I thought we would always be friends, away from whether I thought we were anything more.

I got lost, out walking that first week. Creasing my paper napkin into smaller and smaller folds on the bar, I tell my friend that the streets in Dublin curve and bend, go off at misdirecting angles compared to the grid I knew back in New York. But I felt empowered by what our teacher, Daniel Byrne, had said to me—*No better way exists to get to know a place than being turned around.* But then it grew dark, and I felt rising disorientation, and at every dusky intersection something seemed to loom. I remember Clare began to text me, on the tiny chirping cell phone I'd resented being made to purchase according to the program rules, apparently for situations just like this one.

Just checking, but are you coming back soon?

Of course, I would act like I had meant it, when I found my way back to Devlin Road that night, where Clare and Doolan and Sasha and Lena were watching Irish reality television, a singing competition. I gave a small and convincing performance: I said I'd needed the fresh air and solitude, had meant to walk the quiet parts of the city all alone in growing darkness, all these hours. In a row on the sofa, they nodded and believed me. Perhaps this kind of authority to interpret the meaning of a story is part of why I stayed an extra week in Ireland at the end, stayed to drive out to Dingle in a rented car with Lena and Margo: I wanted time before leaving to make sense of the weeks, to make sense of the story I sensed was already beginning to escape my capacity to interpret it. Besides which, I was reluctant to leave; I had loved the anonymity of this country, of being outside what anyone knew of me at home— loved, too, the heady closeness of being one of the crew at 13 Devlin Road, and the intuitive sense of slightly belonging, in this place where I had distant ancestry.

When I got home I emailed Alice Doolan: *The exact moment of "the end" is devastating in its way, but I always find the gradual drain of something becoming the past is a little bit worse.*

From halfway across the US came her reply. She said she appreciated the exquisite detail of something I said I really missed: running full throttle down the tall, narrow stairway at 13 Devlin, and careening around the corner into the dining room. Much as Doolan herself did, after she heard the fox from her third-floor bedroom and thought it was me who was screaming that way. I told her this was just the kind of thing I linger over, lovingly: the sky turning pink, the city's yellow buses, the sensation of release when you ran down those stairs. The colors, the details: I fixate on their fading sprawl while the plot is getting lost. So I still remember the colors on the first day, when we met to walk to class, gathering at the fork where Rathmines Road diverged, a shop called Little Ass Burrito Bar irreverent at the crossroads: Kevin Harris's sweater was pastel green, James Gallagher's jacket was the color of wet sand, and the air was gray, wooly, looking like rain. Anywhere you go in Ireland, even when you perceive it to be sunny, you must bring an umbrella and wear practical shoes. Things could turn at any moment. Or this is what our RA seemed to be warning us, when she sat with us at Devlin Road on our second day to review program rules and dispense local advice: *Girls, you must always consider what might happen.*

You must think how, in the space of weeks, "to up-question" might become one piece of a brief language you all share—how this language might seem like proof the collective friendship will endure. How you might come to call yourselves the Devlin 13: me, Doolan, Sasha, Lena, and Clare who actually lived at the house, but James and Sam and Harris, too—they lived just a few blocks west, so they were always in our living room. Margo, Toby, Blaise who had a thing for Sasha, Hallie Wolfe in all her intensity, and Nate once we'd warmed up to him, had oriented ourselves to his bravado, his funny ways of talking himself up and then tacking on that consequential "So . . ."

(The "so . . ." that flowered with implication, with possibility, then trailed away to nothing.)

I remember I picked up a five-euro copy of *Ulysses* in a museum bookshop, drawn to the idea of a demanding, inward text, after Daniel Byrne distributed its first chapter, photocopied, at the end of our first class. I arrived at a section called "The Grandeur That Was Rome." (That *was*. Past tense.) "Wait a moment, Professor McHugh said, raising two quiet claws. We mustn't be led away by words, by sounds of words." But who can resist being led away? For that summer, to be one of our crew was to share in certain things. Like drinking cider from glass bottles in the living room, or like the morning some of us stood in the hall before class and each took a bite of my sandwich—Sam, Doolan, Sasha, me. The brevity of shared experience: ham and cheese. Like me and James Gallagher standing outside a theater in Temple Bar, looking at the still-light 10 p.m. sky, sharing a chocolate bar, or me and Alice Doolan in our kitchen, listening for the sound of the crying fox. Dublin was gray and brick, the sky spitting rain on the two-decker yellow buses. The city of Joyce, of roaming consciousness grasping onto time, place, the personal ordering of experience—so personal it might well become opaque, illegible.

One rare sunny afternoon we went to the Chester Beatty Library, then up to its pretty rooftop garden, where Sasha ran to the balustrade and shouted effusively to a couple wrapped around each other on the grass below: *Fuck yeah, kissing rules!* I can't explain why it seemed so funny—can only evoke the sparkle of sharing in the joke, and how we could not stop repeating it: *Fuck yeah, kissing rules.*

By then we had known each other three weeks, and I remember walking home from class one day together, all debating if our program was half over, or whether we had half the summer left—which was the truer perspective? Moreover, which felt better to say, which did not raise the specter of an ending, a rupture? By then we had settled it that "to Hallie Wolfe" a person meant "to cuddle someone publicly, regardless of and/or oblivious to his or her interest in being cuddled." Example of proper usage: *I'm totally Hallie Wolfing you right now*, which is what James would say when we were sitting in the concrete garden at 13 Devlin and he was leaning his forehead weirdly but (I decided, in that moment) probably meaninglessly against my knee. It was four in the morning, we were watching the sun come up.

You mean you were watching the sky sort of lighten, Nate would later correct me. *At that time of the morning you can't see the actual sun from the back steps, so.*

That same night, our last together, Hallie had stayed over on the living-room couch, while Sam slept nearby on the floor, nestled in his prized all-weather sleeping bag. Sam was a boy who climbed walls and hopped fences all over

Dublin in those weeks, a boy who did not think laws about where one could or could not go camping should really be applicable to him. There he is in my memories, delightful and intrepid, game for anything, and providing in retrospect a small gloss on the way boundaries can be so readily trespassed by anyone who really wants something. Intermittently that night, Hallie or Sam would stir in their sleep, and James and I would stop our conversation, turn and try to see them through the clustered, shadowed legs of the dining room chairs—peering. Trying to sort out what we were seeing. Like the homework assignment from Daniel Byrne that went, cryptically, wonderfully: "Choose something you are drawn to. Write about it in detail. Observe until you understand why it interests you, what meaning it holds. Fill a notebook if you need to."

I recall things with a vivid clarity. I comb and paw through details, obsessive. I remember how, drinking one night on the patio behind the pub, I proved I could recite every one of our birthdays: July 20, September 4, October 22, November 6, etc., etc., etc., etc. But I do not have synesthesia, unless you can have it for things besides letters and numbers—like a moment, a feeling, a person, a certain togetherness. Hallie might say, *H is pink*, no question. To some extent she made me nervous with her blunt distinctions, her confidence in the workings of her own mind. I preferred talking at length with James, who confessed to be mystified by his own thoughts and wants and choices, his wishes and their contradictions—James, who expressed uncertainty about seeing anything as it really was. My closest friend in the program, I thought then. Anytime we walked next to one another, deep in conversation, he'd unwittingly reach out to grab my arm, holding on. Later, back at college, I would delete every email he had sent me, an effort to feel less suffocated, to push open some door out of our increasing misunderstanding. And years later Alice Doolan would track down my new email and write to say she lived in New York now, and did I want to meet up, and I would decide not to answer because I felt safer with the memory at arm's length.

I am swirling the ice in my drink as I tell my friend how certain nights that summer, I wrote tentative emails from the darkened kitchen, emails home to an old high school boyfriend while the rest of our house was sleeping, an activity I experienced as somehow illicit. One night, an enormous thumb-sized snail moved in from the garden, slid up the kitchen-table leg, and emerged furtively from behind my laptop, weird and blank. It moved its antennae probingly, and I leapt, silent, from my chair.

Something small and lurking may loom large eventually, could be the lesson in that memory, though I can only say so looking back: you might sit in the dark, catching your breath, and the shadows in an empty room may metamorphose to alarming possibilities.

There was something likewise eerie about the two rolls of pictures I tried to develop after the trip, forty-eight photos: each one came out gray and blurry, vague, obscured. But I still remember much of what I photographed, the things I meant to capture, hoped I might hold on to. St. Stephen's Green, Doolan eating an ice cream, Sam leaping to catch wet green grapes as we chucked them in little trajectories through the air. James, sunlit, kicking a soccer ball with debonair agility. Margo and Lena and Nate lying on the grass being "park people," they said, meaning simply they were sitting in the park. The view down Devlin Road from the second floor, and Blaise in my leather jacket, too small—I was wearing his, big and droopy, while I took the photo. Finally Virginia Woolf, as we dubbed the cat who frequented our doorstep, winking her eyes closed at the camera.

The problem with the real Virginia Woolf, said Daniel Byrne one afternoon, holding forth, was the way she continually wrote off James Joyce. When they were doing the same thing really. I thought about that often, later—the idea of holding against someone what you were equally capable of.

Meanwhile in Daniel Byrne's class, we were permitted only to offer positive feedback on one another's writing. By reading into the gaps of what had not been praised, he said, we might each divine our shortcomings. Perhaps, all summer, this exacerbated my tendency to avoid saying anything uncomfortable to anyone, rather than risk writing over the affection I felt for them. *I love you*, Hallie would say, drunk in the pub, her head on my shoulder. Not once did I ask her to give me some space, not once did I say, *This is too close.* Only one-on-one, in a required conference with each of us at the halfway point of the summer, did Daniel Byrne disclose his unvarnished opinions. Across one of my stories he had written in red pen: *You are blundering your shifts from one point of view to another.*

In the bar on Irving Place, I tell my friend I have no certain explanation for why the photographs didn't develop, but that I think in each possibility, there is a code through which to read the summer. It might be that the old Pentax was broken, in which case there was nothing I could have done, it was a doomed endeavor. Or I could have put my film through the security scanner at the airport when I was crying about going home, in which case it got wiped, a regrettable but innocent mistake. Or from the outset I might have inserted the film incorrectly, not once but twice, and in spite of my awareness of the necessity to double-check. If so, I should have paid attention. Each of the forty-eight times I turned the wheel to bring in the next frame, I should have realized I was doing something wrong; I had every opportunity to notice my mistakes as they accrued. Not unlike the night I insisted we see an experimental film at the cinema center in Temple Bar, which I thought I would enjoy. Instead the rapid-fire splicing of the images became dreadful, spectral, hyperbolic, their accumulation frightening. Having ensnared myself in a mistake of my own making, I covered my eyes in my seat between Doolan and James, whose arm was touching mine. Nate leaned over to say: *I think I love this. I'm not sure though—we'll see.*

My friend is finishing the last of his whiskey, and the napkin I've folded and folded and folded down to a small node of paper rests on the bar between our glasses. He wants to know, What happened to them, do you know? And I say I know only the immediate aftermath: it ended. We all went home again, I to the town outside New York, then back to college, sophomore year. Hallie Wolfe to Palo Alto, Doolan to St. Louis, James to Virginia, etc., etc., etc., etc. Ireland stayed put. In the months that followed, if anyone asked me I'd say, *We keep in touch,* which was already becoming a kind of lie, to suggest I had the story under my control. That nothing about it had begun to upset me, that the memories were not rewriting themselves into a more threatening shape. That I was not ignoring texts from the one named James on principle, because it more and more seemed better to be wordless and unreachable when your interpretations don't line up.

Tonight I tell my friend that, looking back, I find Hallie's questions in the cab were prescient: she was right to raise the specter of misinterpretation, and its danger. Of course this is the opportunity of retrospect, and its trick—but

I can hardly believe I was ever a person to whom such questions didn't matter, when after that they came to frighten me the way they did. I still think often of the first night, in a pub on the canal: James is talking to me with total attentiveness, and I feel alive to everything he has to say. We seem to make easy sense to each other, though also it's like his attention is too much, a room where the light is a little too bright. Then James and I are joined by Hallie Wolfe, and she takes the opportunity of a small lull in our conversation to tell us her beliefs concerning how to offer useful feedback on a story. *You have to try to work within the author's point of view*, she tells us, instructive and cheerful with her shock of pink hair. *You have to help them write the story they are writing, and not the one that you would write yourself from their material. You can only offer feedback through this framework*. And James and I catch one another's eye as she begins to detail her use of colored highlighters to carry out a personal, intricate editing code. *So yellow is for syntax, green is for awkward phrasing. Pink is for a striking image, and blue is for clichés*.

In Ireland, the summer sun rises early and sets well after ten o'clock. By the time we left the pub, the gray clouds had colored magnificently, not unlike the way the word *Hallie* turned pink inside the matter of her brain.

The whole scope of those weeks seems colored now by encroaching closeness, by entitlement. James was always reaching for my elbow, and the thing about being Hallie Wolfed was how it consistently made me squirm—I didn't like being hugged without granting permission, without initiating it myself. I hated the presumptuous closeness, the subtle invasion, it made me shrink. So why was my method reciprocation? Shouting over group karaoke in a sweaty, blue-lit room on Toby's birthday, or drinking cheap pink wine while Blaise turned hot dogs on an improvised foil grill on the Fourth of July, or finally sitting with Hallie on the living-room sofa on one of those last nights, *I love you too*, I responded every time, weary, but meaning it maybe, as she turned her devoted face into the side of my neck. *I love you too.*

Perhaps I only wanted to buy myself time to figure it out later, "it" being the thing I actually meant to say but never discovered.

Or did I reciprocate, in spite of my alarm? Or did I love the feeling of belonging, of being loved?

I told her I loved her back, and then for months I barely had a thing to say in reply when she called me on the phone or sent postcards to my campus mailbox. Likewise I told James on the last night, as the sky lightened, while Hallie who was always too close and Sam who observed no boundaries slept nearby in the living room: *Yes.* Yes, under other less finite and entirely hypothetical circumstances,

I could consider the idea of you, us, in another light, another kind of coloration. I said this as if it were as simple as Hallie choosing to dye her pink hair a new color. Perhaps if we lived in the same place, perhaps if I was not still attached to the ex-boyfriend at home, perhaps if the summer was not ending. Perhaps then I might interpret us another way. Hallie of course would highlight this in green for awkward phrasing. Or blue, for the cliché of knowing this would end, thinking there was no harm in being kind, in evading clearer choices, thinking the story could not be corrupted. Thinking I could do no wrong if I tried only to preserve it as it was. I am always holding on to things at any cost. *Fuck yeah, kissing rules*, I wrote to him at the end, when he was at the airport and I was packing at Devlin Road, thinking the best thing I could offer about what had passed between us that last night was to make this clever reference. I was still in thrall to the shared joke, and it came to me now as a way out: I thought maybe I had kissed him because I was excellent at following Hallie's rules, which is to say, at offering feedback filtered only through someone else's vision and never through my own. I sent him this message on my pay-as-you-go Irish cell phone, which promptly informed me it had run out of credit, and which I never had occasion to use again. So now, removed from there, I am here, in a bar in New York ten years later—unable to locate the lost plot, the source of my own slapdash language, the nesting bowl of intent stacked inside the other four of what

I tried to say and do, did say, did do. Having outgrown the situation by years, in contact with none of them, yet here still with the unresolved story nested inside me, garbled, disorienting. And why do I care anymore? Because the closeness between us all was transforming, made the empty room of who I was then bright and shiny like a holiday, like everyone gathered around a table? Or because that emptiness was easy for James to furnish with a fantasy I didn't want to puncture, hoping he would read my *no* between the lines? Or because after this summer, dread became part of who I was, as if so many shadows reached for my arms, slippery and quiet? As if I was the wordless screaming fox, while his emails accumulated in my inbox, his voicemails on my phone?

There is no resolution, and the rendering of certain details is all I have to give here. I can only say what I saw, felt, absorbed. The color of the sky. Never what I myself wanted, nor my own intentions—never what thing I might have wanted most.

My friend and I have left the bar to smoke out on the sidewalk, and I hear myself describing how I loved the chimneys in relief against the sky, outside our bathroom window there on Devlin Road. How the lightbulb in that room burned out in our first week, so I took showers in the dark all summer. So did Clare, so did Sasha, so did Lena, so did Alice Doolan, in this house we five girls shared. I say it's strange, to no longer know a single person who remembers that: how it was like standing in a dim and misty cave. Then I let my friend hold the lighter to the end of my cigarette, its small glow warm by my face.

Daniel Byrne, at the end of program, marked up another of my stories in red ink and noted the inscrutability of plot, and again my blundering of each shift from one point of view to another—a thing that Joyce or Woolf would never do, engaged as they were in the technical perfection of such shifts.

My clearest shortcomings, he said—and this, too: my evident incapacity to state outright what any character actually desired.

If I could reform these habits, he said, if I could rein in my use of adverbs and stop writing sentences that began with indefinite articles, then I might well get somewhere. And I have not figured out if he was right or wrong. So in this retrospective mode I can do nothing but describe the way it seemed to me, or how it remains now in the picture in my mind, and then try to read some meaning in it: *Gruff, friendly, a little alarming, Daniel Byrne looks across the table at me in the burger place on Portobello Road, points his finger, and growls: "Listen to me, really listen: Every character wants something."*

Everyone wants something, but I only attend to the sur-
rounding details. The wind moves the bare branches on the
small trees planted along this sidewalk in New York. I am
looking at the chilly gleam on every piece of glass in the
architecture of 19th Street where it intersects with Irving.
I am looking at the orange end of my friend's cigarette,
bright in the dark—the evocative, the indelible periphery,
my attention to which is maybe my strange power, the
thing I have to offer, unless it's my obsession, my failure,
my eventual sticking point, the place where my wheels just
start to spin and spin and go on spinning. Would you want
another drink? my friend is asking, smiling. We make easy
sense to each other, there are possibilities before us. I stab
out my cigarette, pull my coat close around me. Yes, I say,
and think how I will one day recollect this night from some
great distance. Yes, sure, why not, let's see.

ACKNOWLEDGMENTS

——— —— ———

To be in collaboration with so many people in the years I wrote this book has meant everything, and I'm grateful I get to say thank you in print.

To my agent, Gráinne Fox, and my editor at Algonquin, Betsy Gleick, thank you for your friendship through this process, for understanding these stories and seeing them into the world, an absolute gift.

Thank you to my teachers, especially Catherine Imbriglio, who made writing possible, and Mary-Beth Hughes, who made a book possible.

So many thanks, for more than I can say, to my sister Maggie, and to my parents, Kevin and Jane. To my two oldest friends, Johana Borjas-Pavon and Maggie Mellor.

To Stephanie Arditte, pure enthusiasm. To Jacob Combs, always my sounding board, willing to edit even my emails. Laura Cresté and Emma Hine, ever dispensing wise advice. Michael Sarinsky, for years of careful line edits and iambic pentameter. Sebastian Doherty and Victoria Kornick, who understood Helen right off the bat. Sophie Netanel for our Kos Kaffe writing days. Linda Harris Dolan, who made time amidst everything (!) to give perspective. James Ciano, encouraging about both short stories and long hair. Sara Brenes Akerman, ultimate reader to turn to with a ghost story. Jennifer Harlan, inspiration for a beloved roommate (luckily one who would never unceremoniously depart). Michelle Ross and Alisa Koyrakh, who weighed in early and invaluably. Alyx Cullen, tarot enthusiast, lighter of candles. Dan Noonan and Steve Potter, the most encouraging appreciators of sentences. Laurel Rhame, for insisting on that one adverb, among many gestures of support. Panpan Song, for a decade of writing friendship.

Thank you to the Angels—some already named here, but also our critic Tess Crain, our star Tess Gunty, our writer-musician Torrey Smith. I'm grateful for all the hours we've spent together, talking about our lives, keeping each other writing. Thank you for being the last set of eyes on the first full draft of this book.

In workshops and writing groups over the years, thank you to everyone who gave essential feedback: too many of you to name, but I'm grateful. Particular thanks to the women of Mary-Beth's generative workshop, and to my grad school cohort at NYU, for an experience of such belonging and community.

Thank you to the journals that featured some of these stories; there would be no book without the encouragement and edits I had from *Meridian*, *Bodega*, *Pigeon Pages*, *ANMLY*, *Cordella*, *Wigleaf*, *Electric Literature*, *A Public Space*, and *Split Lip*. Thanks especially to T Kira Madden, Molly Tolsky, and *No Tokens*. And to Hannah Beresford, for brilliant insights at a key moment.

Thank you to the residencies that brought me into community with other artists, and to the program staff whose work makes those spaces possible. Thank you to my fellow residents at the Adirondack Center for Writing, for all the warmth and fun: Jane Boxall, Erin Dorney, Kelsey Francis, Allison Strack, and Emily Weitzman. Thanks also to those I met at Virginia Center for the Creative Arts, generous with your friendship as I was making the last round of edits.

This book is in part about looking for home, and I'm grateful for the places that became mine while I was writing it—first New York City and later Ithaca. Thank you especially to Emily Powell and Jack Hartman, Celine and Joe Cammaratta, Becky Bailey and Josh Del Rio, Madeleine

Barnes, Elena Aleksandrovna, and Chris Dolan. Many, many thanks to Erica Shockley. At Buffalo Street Books in Ithaca, a home in and of itself, thank you to Lisa, Carmen, Charles, Isis, Ivy, Nesiah, and Oliver: for covering for me when I went to residencies, for always welcoming me right back, for generally embracing me and my writing and my Luna. (Extra thanks to Oliver and Christine for above-and-beyond dog sitting during those residencies.) And thank you to the Community Arts Partnership of Tompkins County: every writer should have such meaningful support from the place they call home.

Thank you to the team at Algonquin, including Jovanna Brinck, Laura Essex, Steve Godwin, Brunson Hoole, Ashley Mason, Mae Zhang McCauley, Stephanie Mendoza, Lizzi Middleman, Christopher Moisan, Travis Smith, Chris Stamey, and many others—for taking such care with my writing, for including me so meaningfully in the details of turning a manuscript into a book. Thank you to Jennifer Savran Kelly: I'm beyond grateful for whatever bit of magic and fate put both of us in Ithaca, both our books at Algonquin. In the UK, thank you to my editor Olivia Hutchings, and to everyone at Corsair.

Thank you to Cassie Mannes Murray, who read this in a day and said yes to working together, who has been an extraordinary advocate for these stories—and to Zoe-Aline

Howard, who was right on board with her. Thank you to Kelly Karzewksi, who takes care of all the details. To Hannah Church for giving voice to these stories. To Tyler Barton, for a warm introduction. To Sarah Dean, for her eagle eyes. To Coco Mellors, for encouragement when I most needed it.

Thank you to the writers whose extraordinarily generous words appear on the jacket of this book; your kindness lifted me up completely.

There is no simple way to say thank you to Amanda, to Ann, or to Stacey, but thank you. And thank you to Simone, who said we should just take a moment, who believed there would be a book, and who, I have to think, pointed the way to Amsterdam. Thank you to Paulette Pettorino, who is like family, who steadied me on through my twenties. Thank you to my beloved extended family. And thank you to the Sanchezes, for your enthusiasm along this path to a book.

Thank you to sweet Luna for your company! All the dogs in this book foreshadowed your arrival on the scene. And thank you and then some to Andy—once a new friend to whom I emailed, late at night, the first pages I ever wrote about Helen, because we had a workshop deadline looming, and we were trying to encourage each other. Thank you for reading those pages with characteristic generosity and perceptiveness. For getting it about the earrings, and for believing in this book ever since. I'm glad I spend my days with you. Not a compliment, just a fact.

And to everyone who reads this book: thank you.